The Horton Chronicles

How Horton Becomes a Hero

First paperback edition December 2019

Book design and illustrations by Anthony Lyng

ISBN 978-1-9163297-0-6

Dedication

For our grandchildren and their parents and our friends Chris and Anita.

Without their antics the story of Horton would not have been possible.

GENESIS

In the corner of the car park, there stands a life size wooden sculpture of two boxing hares.On closer inspection, you will see an inscription;

HORTON AND HIS BFF MORTON.

FOR SAVING SIR THOMAS BUNGLEBURY.

Find out and decide for yourself whether Horton and his BFF Morton, are worthy of this dedication.

Follow the adventures of Horton, together with his crew of trusted and loyal friends.

Are Horton's escapades, along with help from his companions and the inhabitants at The Hall, raising the profile of Bunglebury Hall and the

small village of Bunbury?

Are they deserving of their description in the

prestigious Waytogo.com website as a place of

interest to visit?

Part One

SPLASH!

The four Town Council workers dropped their tools and stood transfixed as the green fisherman's hat floated downstream on a slow moving island of weeds and grass.

"What?"..........

Chapter One

Horton's Plan

Horton had made a decision.

He looked up at the orange, red and violet colours of the twilight sky.

Yes!

Tomorrow would be a good day for a trek. "Red sky at night, shepherd's delight!" he thought to himself.

Being a very conscientious and careful person, he also checked the three weather apps. on his mobile phone: Sunny with a few clouds; no rain; a temperature of twenty degrees. All three apps agreed!

It would definitely be a good day for a trek.

And who better to accompany him than his BFF Morton?

Morton had been his BFF since they were babes in prams, and where Horton went, Morton usually went too. Service on Horton's mobile phone was intermittent as both he and Morton lived in the woods, but he knew he could rely on The Robinettes to take a message to Morton first thing in the morning. They were always delighted to pass messages to Horton's friends. Horton always had great ideas and it was exciting to be part of his team.

As he nestled down under his red and white check duvet, he thought about the trek. It would be fun to go and see their friend Ernestine again. They would take their favourite foods. Horton quickly fell asleep dreaming about juicy blackberries, gummy bears, chocolate biscuits and cordial.

The Robinettes woke Horton with their melodious singing to greet the day which had dawned bright and sunny. Horton leapt out of bed and stretched. He threw back his red and white check curtains and flung open the window to chat to his friends. Could they take a message to his friend Morton? It would be a lovely day for a trek.

How could he know that this was the day his life was going to change forever?

How could he know that by the end of the day he would be hailed a hero for saving the life of Sir Thomas Bunglebury, owner of The Hall?

While The Robinettes flew over to pass on Horton's message to his best friend, Horton prepared himself for the day ahead.

No.5, Willow Wood Cottages, Horton's home, was always neat, clean and tidy. Everything has a place and everything is in its place. There are red and white check curtains at the windows, a red and white check tablecloth with a red vase of red and white flowers on the table, and thick red cushions on his comfortable chair. Upstairs his very comfortable, neatly made bed has red and white check bedclothes. His home is very red and very neat and tidy.

You would expect Horton, our Hero, to also be very neat and tidy.

Quite the opposite.

He does his very best but can't seem to get it right. His hair is always out of place. No amount of brushing or combing can make his grey, shaggy, standy-uppy hair lie flat and the fact that one ear will not stand up straight but falls over half way makes it even more difficult. A problem since birth, no amount of physiotherapy, splints or any other medical treatment could disguise the fact that he had one loppy ear and one straight uppy one, so everyone knew who Horton was. Despite his physical appearance, Horton always started the day very clean. He brushed his teeth regularly so there was no plaque on them; he showered daily; he used his deodorant to make sure he smelled nice; his clothes were always clean every day; but, unfortunately by the end of the day he would always look rather messy. This was always due to events which occurred during the day, usually helping others out rather than doing his own chores .

As the Robinettes flew off, Horton dressed himself in his red shorts and red T shirt, tied his red bandanna with white spots around his head, (he couldn't wear a hat because of his one lop sided ear} and prepared his red 'Just in Case' rucksack. Into this he put a First Aid Kit, flask of cordial, some biscuits, chocolate biscuits wrapped in tin foil to keep them cool, and a container of his favourite juicy blackberries which he had picked the previous day. Also, he had a packet of little gummy bears, just in case he and Morton had the munchies. His 'Just in Case' red rucksack also contained a compass {in case he got lost}, some strong cord,{never know when it might come in handy} and an Acme Thunderer whistle {in case he needed to attract attention}.

 The Robinettes returned as Horton finished his preparations.

 Yes! Morton was definitely up for a trek.

Leaving 5, Willow Wood Cottages immaculately clean and tidy, Horton hurried off to meet his BFF Morton.

His Best Friend Forever Morton was just the opposite to Horton. He never had a hair out of place as he used lots of product on it. His face was never exposed to the vagaries of the weather as Horton's was. as he spent time in front of his bathroom mirror applying moisturiser. He was also very particular as regard to his personal hygiene, brushing his teeth regularly and showering daily etc. Clean blue clothes were worn daily. But even doing the dirtiest work, Morton appeared as clean and fresh at the end of the day as when he started it. Unfortunately, the same could not be said of his home at 9, Dingley Dell Woodlands.

With an address like that you would imagine his home to be like that of Horton's, and, indeed from the outside it looked very cosy with a very attractive wooden front door with a brass knocker on it. There the resemblance to Horton's home ended, for as you entered it, it was the most untidy place imaginable. The blue and white check curtains were never pulled across neatly, there were always crumbs on the blue and white tablecloth and Morton always forget to refresh the fading blue turned brown flowers in the blue vase. His sagging armchair always needed the blue cushions to be plumped up, and when he went upstairs to his bedroom, he never had time to make his bed. He was always far too busy putting product on his hair, or moisturising his face and then leaving his pots and potions all around his house.

Morton was almost ready to go. He was wearing his blue shorts and T shirt and a blue back to front baseball cap with holes in it to allow his ears to stand up straight. His blue 'Everything in It' rucksack was full of really useful stuff: small screwdriver and socket set; puncture repair kit; sewing set; small set of useful screws, nuts and bolts; torch; and bicycle pump. Horton could never undertsand why his best friend always carried such a heavy, Everything In It rucksack, but he supposed its contents might come in useful one day. Morton also included another packet of gummy bears, in case they had more munchies. All he needed to do was finish moisturising his face as his BFF Horton swiftly tidied around a bit, and they were ready to go.

"I hoped you fancied a bit of a trek" he said, "I was thinking it's such a beautiful day and we haven't seen our friend Ernie the Sheep for ages!"

Ernestine the sheep lived high on a mountain and was the furthest away of all their friends. She like their other friend Corwen a black Dexter cow (who ranged from field to field) when messaged by The Robinettes to attend a meeting for an Important Happening, would always find a way to reach Horton.

They did not see Ernie or Corwen on a regular basis, but Horton and Morton valued their friendship and loyalty, and knew they would always support them in any situation, good and bad. It would be good to catch up with Ernie, and they might also see Corwen on the way.

Like the best friends they were, Horton and Morton set off on their trek chatting and laughing, enjoying the fresh air and sunshine, oblivious to anything else and intent upon their visit to Ernestine.

Chapter Two

Sir Thomas Bunglebury's Plan

Sir Thomas Bunglebury looked out of The Hall's kitchen window as he was eating his breakfast of boiled egg and 'soldiers' – strips of buttered toast ideal for dipping in an egg.

"I've decided it's such a beautiful day, I'll go fishing on the canal. Is that alright with you, Milady?"

His wife's name was actually Melody, but Sir had always pronounced it Milady, and the name had stuck.

Milady folded her newspaper and looked at him "That's nice, dear! I'll ask Mrs. Keeper to prepare a picnic lunch for you."

"And I'll ask Mr. Keeper to get the boat out."

Sir and Milady lived in The Hall. It had been in Sir's family for generations, a reward from Queen

Elizabeth the First for services rendered by an ancestor, his namesake Sir Thomas Bunglebury, during The Spanish Armada. Owing to the improper placement of a cannon aboard his ship, The Silver Goose, Sir Thomas Bunglebury had accidentally fired an enormous cannon ball in the wrong direction. By some fluke, this cannon ball had changed direction mid air and landed on the deck in the middle of the explosives stockpiled on board the Spanish Armada's Fleet Admiral's galleon. The cannon ball had exploded on impact sending fireballs into the air and onto the pile of explosives which had caused fire to rain down, not only on that galleon killing the Admiral and many Spanish sailors, but catching alight other Spanish ships which were in the vicinity. As a result of this action, The Spanish Armada had turned tail and limped away across the English Channel. Sir Thomas Bunglebury was welcomed as a saviour of the British Navy and great defender of England by that great British seafarer, Sir Francis Drake, thereby being rewarded for services rendered to The Crown in the form of this estate, Bunglebury Hall, or The Hall as the locals called it, and its accompanying lands.

The present Sir Thomas, generally just known as Sir, would have loved to be the owner of a garage, as he loved tinkering with cars, particularly vintage cars. Unfortunately for him, it was incumbent upon him to maintain the upkeep of the property which had been in the Bunglebury family for centuries.

As the name suggests, the Bunglebury family had an infliction which had been passed down the generations: sometimes even their most well intentioned acts turned into complete disasters. Taking care of this large estate involved a tremendous amount of work. Wisely, for once, this Sir Thomas Bunglebury had gathered around him some excellent people who could be relied upon to help with its upkeep.

Milady, his wife, oversaw the daily upkeep of The Hall. Not only did she do the accounts and look after the financial affairs, but she was also instrumental in village affairs, being on the committees of a large number of village groups and societies.

Centuries earlier, the village had grown up around The Minster Church and, later, The Hall. The villagers were so proud of their new neighbour, they had decided to change the village name to one which would reflect their pride. However, they did not want the connotations of the name of Bunglebury to be shared with them, fearing it would have an adverse effect on their economy. It was shortened to Bunbury and the villagers at that time agreed to change the name of their traditional fruity cakes to Bunbury Buns. Like Bakewell Tarts and Eccles Cakes, Bunbury Buns were synominous with the village, and over the years, fortunes had been made from the sale of these scrumptious cakes.

Mr. Keeper looked after the estate and lands, while his wife Mrs.Keeper was in charge of the daily tasks and was particularly busy in the kitchen. Her cooking was second to none,and the kitchen was probably the most frequented room in the house, filled as it was with the most delicious of smells and warmth.

Mr. and Mrs. Keeper had their own cottage, Keeper's Lodge, near the entrance gate to The Hall. Mr. Keeper was a formidable man: he could be scary if you did something not right or something he disapproved of, but he was also formidable because he had so much knowledge. He knew everything, literally everything, if you wanted to know about astronomy, he would show you the stars and the sky at night through his telescope; if you wanted to know how to tie up runner beans, he would show you a range of knots to use; if you wanted to know which bird made which song, he would know. He could recite and write poetry, could perform speeches from Shakespeare's Julius Caesar or Hamlet; and what he didn't know from his wealth of experience, would work with you to find a solution to your problem, using Google or You Tube and even old fashioned books! He wasn't an imposing character as he was neither short nor tall; thin nor fat; he looked friendly and kind with his balding head, ruddy complexion and horn rimmed spectacles; but woe betide you if you got on the wrong side of him. Scary!

So, that beautiful morning, following Sir's instructions, Mr. Keeper made his way down to the rickety old boathouse on the banks of the becalmed lake in front of The Hall. He unlocked it, hoping the rusty keys wouldn't stick in the old lock; charged up the battery on the six-seater electric boat; ensured the lifebelt, pole, mooring ropes and other paraphernalia required for the smooth running of a day's fishing on the canal were on board; and everything was ready. Sir was bringing the ancient fishing rod which had belonged to his grandfather, as well as the rusted old tin of fishing flies .

But where was Sir?

Mrs. Keeper, a kindly lady who looked just as you might imagine she would {being married to Mr. Keeper and being an excellent cook} was neat, rosy cheeked, grey haired, slightly rotund and always wearing an apron. There was nothing she liked more than preparing a feast, so when Milady had asked her to provide a picnic for Sir's fishing trip, she had, of course, gone to town. Not literally, of course, but she had prepared a stack of delicious victuals for the picnic hamper. There were pork pies, scotch eggs, chicken drumsticks, ham, cheese, cherry tomatoes and salads and cucumber and carrot slices; brown bread rolls, soft white rolls, cheesy topped rolls and her renowned Green Tomato Chutney. There were bags of crisps- cheese and onion, salt and vinegar, barbecue and salted. There was fruit - bananas, apples, tangerines, and grapes. And to drink she had put in flasks of coffee, tea and bottles of pink lemonade and cordial. There was enough food to feed not only Sir, but all the people who lived on the barges which were moored alongside the canal banks.

Finally, Mrs Keeper placed knives, forks, spoons and paper glasses and napkins into the enormous wicker picnic hamper and shouted to Sir that his picnic was ready.

Mr. Keeper had returned to The Hall to find out what the delay was.

Now he understood! He struggled to the boat with the massive hamper and placed it under one of the benches. The boat sank at least five centimetres down into the water.

Finally, Sir arrived dressed in his green fishing gear - green wellington boots, green dungarees and checked shirt, sunglasses and green fishing hat; carrying the old fishing rod which his grandfather had used, and his old metal box filled with different flies (not the insects, but the ones fishermen used to make to catch different fish).

Mr. Keeper handed him another box.

Sir opened it and grimaced, "Yuk!"

"Maggots, Sir. Just in case the old-fashioned flies don't work!"

As he helped Sir into the electric boat, reaching out to stop Sir's fishing hat from falling into the lake, Sir whistled for one of his dogs to accompany him. Digby, one of the two black Labrador twins, leapt into the boat, making it rock violently to and fro for a few minutes. When it had settled, and after a few instructions from Mr. Keeper on gears, braking, reversing and going forward and how to get rid of weeds which could jam the propeller, Sir started the engine and slowly pushed off from the bank and headed towards the canal.

Now for a day's calm and peaceful fishing.

Chapter Three

The Trek

The paths Horton and Morton followed led them up a mountain track which climbed higher and higher. Looking down, they could occasionally see the route of the canal as it cut its path from The Hall's lake through the village of Bunbury and on through the countryside to the industrial hub of the area. Many years had passed since then, and now it was used solely for leisure and pleasure.

Up, up, higher and higher they climbed jauntily. Horton's red 'Just in Case' rucksack was swung over one shoulder, while Morton's 'Everything in It' rucksack was carried firmly on his back. Having walked for quite some time, Morton was getting slower and slower. It was quite hot, after all, and he didn't have the enormous feet that Horton had.

"I'm tired "he moaned. "Can't we sit for a while? "

He found a flat granite rock to sit on, delved deep into his blue 'Everything in It' rucksack, and pulled out a packet of gummy bears. He offered some to Horton and there they sat munching happily, their eyes scanning the horizon for any sign of Ernie the Sheep. There was no sign of Ernestine, but from this vantage point they had a great view of the lake and the canal. They watched a small blue dot with two shapes inside, steadily make its way over the lake and into the canal.

Their eyes glued to this vision, they did not see large black Dexter cow sporting a multi coloured rainbow scarf to which, hanging down the front of her neck like a necklace, was attached a row of small copper coloured cowbells, come rambling towards them. The bells made a loud melodious sound and disturbed their reveries.

It was Corwen!

The two BFF's had not seen their other friend Corwen for a long time and they were delighted by this chance meeting.

"How do" uttered Corwen. " Long time, no see, but great to catch up with you now!"

The friends chatted for a while and then Corwen told them about the race she had just devised for her Bovinettes.

There were fifteen of them, each looking exactly alike, large, ponderous and very black, but of varying size and age. except for Corwen, distinguishable only by her multi coloured rainbow scarf and cowbells.

"Now you're here, could you give us Starters' Orders, please Horton?"

She fluttered her long black eyelashes and looked at Horton with her large, limpid dark eyes.

How could Horton refuse ?

Horton looked up and down. There were eleven black cows in a horizontal line at the top of the field. At the bottom of the field, lying in a vertical row, their front legs crossed over each other, were three older grandmother black Dexter cows, gossiping to each other and looking eagerly up at the line of cows at the top. Corwen ambled over and joined the line. Horton and Morton's mouths opened wide in astonishment.

Corwen winked her long black eyelashes at Horton, who felt deep into his 'Just In Case' rucksack.

He pulled out his Acme Thunderer, "I see the umpires down below are ready" he announced.

Inhaling a deep breath, he blew a piercing whistle on his Acme Thunderer.

Thinking it was a bit of a joke, the two BFF's could not believe their eyes as the cows started to run, slowly at first, picking up pace as they dashed down the mountain, leaping over granite boulders as they went. Faster and faster, the line thinning out, some in front, some behind. OH! And one has gone down, and now she's rolling, roly-poly down the mountain field. It's a race. There's no stopping till the bottom is reached.

The elderly Dexter grandmother umpires looked sternly at the competitors. There should be no cheating, so one cow was disqualified for pushing and shoving; one needed attention for a sprained ankle, one needed a shock for hiccups as she'd laughed so much from rolypolying down, and there was one outright winner.

"Thanks," mouthed Corwen, as Horton and Morton were still staring open mouthed at the amazing scene just played out before them.

"Well I never "said Horton. "If I hadn't seen it with my own eyes, I would never have believed it!"

Still chuckling in amazement, the two friends went on their way to find Ernie the Sheep once more, having taken one last glance down at the lake and canal where the blue dot seemed to be stationary. It must be passing through the lock.

Slinging their rucksacks over their shoulders, the two BFF's began climbing up the mountain again. It was hot and hard work. When they reached the plateau near the summit, they looked down to see how far they had climbed. There below them in the valley they could follow the blue speck on the canal, moving very slowly.

They trudged along the flat path on the plateau until they reached a roughly built stone wall. Climbing over, the two friends found a couple of flat rocks where they could eat their next few munchies. The juicy blackberries stained their mouths and chocolatey crumbs clung to their whiskers as their eyes scanned the fields for Ernie.

"She must be here somewhere!" they exclaimed. Suddenly Horton's hawk eyes spotted the tell-tale straw hat on a mass of white fluffiness.

"There she is! Two fields' away!" There a flock of sheep was plodding across the field in a Follow My Leader way, one behind the other. And at the rear could be seen a bit of a slow coach, wearing a straw hat.

Ernie, or to give her full name, Ernestine, was a very important sheep. You would think that because she was always last in the flock that she must be a daydreamer with her head always in the clouds.

Not at all!

She was always last because she was looking after The Stragglers of the flock, who would have surely got lost had Ernie not been behind them, watching out for them. Also, everyone knew who Ernestine was because she stood apart from the rest of the flock as the only sheep who wore a straw hat. It was a very pretty hat, abandoned by a rambler who had forgotten to put it back on her head whilst walking in the mountains one hot, sunny day. Ernie had picked it up and tied it under her chin, so that it could not blow away. She loved this hat: it shaded the sun from her eyes; kept her head warm in cold weather; prevented her head getting wet in the rain; and in spring or summer she could adorn it with flowers to make it look even prettier.

She was in the process of hurrying along a couple of stragglers when Horton and Morton bounded up to her. It had been some time since they had seen each other, so they were all delighted to be in each other's company. It was all very calm and peaceful except for the skylarks singing high above them, and in the distance they could hear the hum of machinery, a mower of some sort they thought.

The stragglers were thirsty though, so it was decided that they would all make their way down to the bottom field where there was access to a flat bank at the side of the canal. Horton and Morton were quite happy to go with them: they weren't in a hurry, and they could take the path alongside the canal to go back home.

The earth was quite muddy down there and Horton and Morton had to hold back some overhanging branches for the sheep to get through. The stragglers lowered their heads in the water and took a long drink. Horton and Morton helped them make their way back up into the field and returned to find Ernie splashing her legs in the cool water.

Chapter Four

Sir almost drowns!

The peace was suddenly violently disturbed by a low buzzing noise which was growing louder and louder. As the noise came closer it was accompanied by clouds of dust and bits of green stuff flying up into the air. Four men came into view wearing bright yellow gilets with Town Council written on the back in bold black lettering. One had a brush cutter, one had a strimmer, one pushed a lawnmower and one carried a sweeping brush. They were clearing tall weeds and grasses from the towpath and the banks of the canal, which would make it easier for cyclists and walkers to use the towpath.

Suddenly the friends heard a loud commotion upstream, coming from the direction from which the workmen had appeared. Ernie stopped splashing and all three jerked their heads in that direction.

The tiny boat which Horton and Morton had seen from the top of the mountain was drifting downstream. Digby, Sir's black Labrador, was excitedly turning round in circles, rocking the boat from side to side while Sir was leaning ominously over the back of the boat.

The three friends could hear Sir talking to himself "Right, engine's stopped, gears neutral, now lean over back of boat, reach down to propeller, clear debris and rubbish away."

As he reached over the back of the boat, his hat fell off and floated away.

"Argh......!"

Digby, ever intelligent, realised what was going to happen as Sir overbalanced as he leaned over.

He grabbed hold of one of Sir's green wellingtons, which dropped from his foot as Digby held it in his mouth.

And with a loud SPLASH, Sir fell headlong into the water.

Horton, ever ready, had been watching this and was thinking at the same time. "Throw in the life jacket! " he yelled at Digby, as the boat drifted opposite them. But Digby's throw missed its target and landed on Ernie's hat. She already had her legs in the water, where she had been cooling herself in the cooling water of the canal.

"Swim, swim to Sir!" Horton shouted, and without thinking and with no time to be frightened, Ernie paddled herself out to Sir.

"Thank you!" he spluttered as he jerked the life jacket from her head and grasped hold of it.

Meanwhile, the workmen had heard the commotion from further down the canal, and came racing along the towpath, heaving a long pole from their van as they did so. Stretching the pole out over the canal, Sir grabbed hold of it and the men pulled Sir to safety.

Sir was furious: in fact, he was so angry his face turned red and then blue. He blamed the men for the accident; the fact that they hadn't cleaned the mess up as they went along, but let it all build up and cause problems for boats in the canal. How many people had fallen overboard because of their stupidity? He couldn't possibly be the only person this had happened to!

"We were told to chop it down, not collect it! But we will give you a ride home in the back of the van!" they said. They felt that this was a reasonable course of action, despite his angry words.

So, dripping wet, feeling quite chilled and very miserable, they loaded him into the back of their truck and left.

Meanwhile, the electric boat was still drifting with Digby on board and Ernestine clinging to the back.

 Horton had been thinking: "We must get on that boat and help!", so giving Morton one end of the piece of strong cord he had in his red 'Just in Case' rucksack, he gave Morton an enormous shove and Morton landed in the boat.

Then with a giant leap himself, Morton and Digby both held onto the other end of the strong cord, and, as if in a tug of war, pulled and pulled and heaved and heaved until Horton found himself collapsed in a heap at the base of the boat., which rocked perilously in the water.

This now left only Ernestine to be saved, as she was lumbering about in the water, trying to hold onto her straw hat and prevent it from getting wet. They grabbed hold of her soggy fleece. Ernie was now weighing at least twice her original weight. They heaved and pulled, pulled and heaved and finally they hefted her into the electric boat, which sank down into the canal, just about still floating. At last, not letting go of her straw hat, Ernie was safely aboard.

"And now what do we do?"

By this time, Sir had been unceremoniously deposited, still dripping wet, chilled and miserable, and covered with weeds and debris, on the grounds in front of The Hall. The workmen roared away in their van, laughing hilariously at the monster they had rescued from the deep.

Milady and Mrs. Keeper almost laughed themselves at the monstrosity of Sir, but feeling sorry for him, they made him take off his wet clothes, wrapped him in a furry blanket and sat him in front of the warm oven in the kitchen. Mrs. Keeper made him a mug of chocolate into which she put a spoonful of brandy, to stop him from getting a cold. Milady went and ran him a hot bath with lots of calming bubble bath.

When he came down from his bath, feeling warm, clean and comfortable again, he immediately phoned up the town council to moan about his exploits, while Milady and Mrs. Keeper tutt-tutted around him.

None of them gave a thought to what had happened to the boat.

Chapter Five

What to do with an Empty Boat?

Horton and his friends had found themselves drifting in the boat with Digby, one of Sir's twin black labradors. No one else had accompanied Sir on the fishing trip, so Horton decided that Digby, therefore, should take charge of the boat.

Digby's chest swelled with pride. Now everyone would find out what a very intelligent black Labrador he was. He had attentively listened to all Mr. Keeper's instructions and as, in all the commotion, the weeds had been disentangled from the boat's propeller, all he needed to do was turn the key, press a button, put the boat in gear, and the boat was in controlled motion again.

Well almost!

It did swing from side to side as Digby practiced steering, but he soon got the hang of it and they all decided it was too good an opportunity to miss out having some fun on the canal for the rest of the day.

Ernie stretched out on the back seat to dry off her fleece in the sunshine, Digby oversaw manoeuvres, so Horton and Morton could relax. Morton discovered the old tin by the fishing rod, which fortunately, had not fallen out of the boat. He opened the tin and there were the old fishing flies to attach to the rod. He couldn't work out how to do this, as he'd never been fishing before, so he closed the tin lid and put them down. Then Horton espied the other newer tin which Mr. Keeper had given Sir.

"I wonder what's in this box", and as he pulled off the lid he screamed" UGH! Maggots!"

He dropped the tin into the canal. It didn't take long for a shoal of fish to appear alongside the boat. There was no need for the fishing rod: all they had to do was put the keep net in the water and they caught enough fish for everyone to have a barbecue later.

 As they were loading the fish into the boat, Horton caught sight of a large wicker basket tucked under a seat. He had felt his tummy rumbling and had suggested that they might all be feeling a bit peckish, and it just so happened they were within sight of the only Inn on the banks of the canal.

 But he was curious, and wanted to know what was inside the basket. Digby stopped the boat and he, Ernie and Morton looked on apprehensively while Horton unstrapped the buckles on the hamper.

"Hope it's not more maggots! "Ernie said worryingly.

What a surprise when Horton lifted the lid!

Their eyes widened in amazement: they had never seen such an enormous amount of food for a picnic in their lives.

Horton thought quickly. "If we don't eat it, all this food will go to waste! And that would be a terrible shame!"

Digby started the boat again, and with a bit of a zig and some zag, the boat finally came to a stop at the canalside Inn. Morton leapt onto the bank with the ropes and moored it safely. Horton passed the picnic hamper to him, Digby helped Ernie, who was now completely dry and looking very clean from her bath in the canal, and they all went up onto the picnicking area on the grass outside the Inn.

Horton delved into his red 'Just in Case' rucksack and found enough money to buy them all some cordial; he thought it wise to do this so that the

Inn's owner wouldn't mind them having a picnic there. Out came the plates, cutlery and napkins, then the plastic glasses were arranged. Then came the food: the pork pies, Scotch eggs, chicken drumsticks, salads, crisps, fruits and jellies, and the assorted drinks. What a feast!

When they had devoured the last chicken drumstick and every crumb, they were all full to bursting. The only thing left was the drink in the thermos flasks.

Digby let out a really loud burp "Oh, excuse me!"

They all lay down on the grass unable to move, they were so full.

Digby's snoring woke Horton with a start. How long had they all slept for? The sun had moved across the sky. It must be time to head back!

Gathering all the picnic paraphernalia together, the four headed down to the boat, and slowly started on their return journey. It took Digby a little time to get accustomed to the controls again, occasionally putting the boat into reverse and then lurching forward but eventually, after a bit of zigzagging, they were eventually properly on their way.

Their first stop was to drop Ernie off. Horton leapt onto the bank and helped her out of the boat.

"Thanks for all your help today! It could have been a different outcome if you weren't here."

"It was exciting! I've never had a day like this before! " she replied.

The stragglers were still waiting for her at the bottom of the field. Naturally they wanted to hear about all the day's exploits. They had heard the commotion, but their view had been obscured by the trees. Horton could see Ernie chatting away to them as they went off to catch up with the rest of the flock. No doubt Ernestine would be an even more important sheep now: she was a heroine!

The little electric boat chugged on along the canal. Horton and Morton were surprised how far they had trekked earlier, as the view up the mountain from the canal looked so different from the scene down from the top of the mountain. Digby was very careful to avoid floating pieces of weed and debris so it was quite a laborious journey past all the large barges moored by the marina.

They stopped to play with Mrs. Quackers and her Quackerlings, who were having a game of hide and seek in the pieces of grass along the bank. Mrs. Quackers was quite upset because she kept counting her brood, but there was always one or two missing. Making waves in the water by reversing and then going forward, the

Quackerlings started a new game of surfing on the ripples, and wore themselves out.

Next stop for the three in the boat was the lock. Horton and Morton, of course, had never experienced this before. Digby, who was a very intelligent black Labrador, had come this way with Sir and had taken everything in, and knew what had to be done. Giving Horton some instruction, he jumped out of the boat holding the key to the lock.

"I'll open the lock gates and Horton you must steer the boat in to the ladder. Put the rope through the side and then hold on tight."

As the water rushed in, Horton and Morton held on very, very tightly as the little boat bounced up and down and swayed backwards and forwards. The green, slimy walls of the lock loomed vertically above them. They were terrified. Eventually the rush of water stopped, the whooshing noise subsided and only a trickle of water entered the lock. The boat came to almost a standstill at the top. They both took a very deep breath. Phew! They felt safe!

"When I've opened the gates, move the boat forward very slowly. I'll come around and we can be on our way again!" Digby ordered.

From then on, it was just plain sailing until they got back to the boathouse at The Hall. There was a reception committee waiting for them as the lockkeeper had phoned ahead. At first, they were really worried that they would be told off, but, no. Sir, Milady, Mr. and Mrs. Keeper, and even Ted the Gardener were all waiting for them. They were all smiling, clapping and cheering. All three, and Ernestine, were the heroes of the moment, especially Horton, whose quick thinking had really saved the day.

Sir proposed a big celebration for them all.

Chapter Six

The Hero

As soon as Sir had received the call from the lockkeeper to say that his boat was being sailed back by that black Labrador and two pals, Sir had immediately decided to show his appreciation to the four who had saved him from drowning.

 He was going to have a celebration at The Hall the following Sunday afternoon.

A platform stage was erected on the front lawn and all the locals were invited. Mrs. Keeper happily provided their favourite foods, which she had discovered were pork pies, Scotch eggs, chicken drumsticks, delicious salads, cold meats, cakes, jellies, fruits, especially blackberries, and huge platefuls of chocolate biscuits. To drink there was plenty of cordial and lemonade, as well as teas and coffees.

All Horton's friends were invited. The Robinettes had been busy taking invitations. Their most important message had been to inform Ernie of the celebration; and she was to meet Digby and Mr. Keeper at the drinking spot on the canal so that they could bring her to the party. (Mr. Keeper wanted to go with Digby to make sure his ability at steering was not a flash in the pan, and that he could really be trusted with the boat. Also, it was easier to get through the lock with two on board.)

Hardip arrived from his home, Hatter's House in the next village,wearing his orange helmet and orange sash, on his orange bike. Hardip was very clever and could always be relied upon to come up with great inventions. Horton often asked for his advice when trying out something new, and Hardip would work alongside Morton when Horton's ideas were turned into reality. He travelled quickly for someone so small: always on his little orange bike, brown, round spectacles perched on the tip of his nose, his orange helmet and orange diagonal sash easily observable from a distance.

Pinkie came in her best Princess gown, looking very pink and very beautiful. She had been named Pinkerton, as her parents were avid readers of detective novels, and had decided to call their next son after one of America's most famous detective agencies.They had laughed when their daughter was born, a girl was an unexpected addition to their male dominated family. Pinkie, as she was now known, was a close neighbour of Horton's, living at 17, Tree Tops, the youngest of a family with seven brothers. She would escape to the peace and calmness of Horton's home from the noisy and cramped family house. Pinkie had a great imagination and loved dressing up, often providing the costumes for Horton and friends for their many fancy dress parties.

The Tweets bounced up and down excitedly and swooped and dived and performed their acrobatics.

Corwen had managed to leave her Bovinettes to attend the celebration. She always looked very dashing in her beautiful rainbow coloured scarf, and her copper cowbell necklace shone more brightly and sounded more melodious than ever as she stood close to the platform.

Ernestine was looking her best in her fluffed up and very clean white fleece, her straw hat tied under her chin and adorned with a beautiful white daisy.

Sir invited her up onto the stage first and thanked her so much for saving his life that her face started to turn red with embarrassment. He presented her with a pink and gold rosette which she was to wear in her hat on very special occasions.

Then it was Morton's turn. He didn't feel that he'd done very much really, but he had had a great day and had been there to shout words of encouragement and moor the boat. He went up onto the stage wearing blue shorts, blue long sleeved shirt and blue and white spotted dicky bow. His hair had been smoothed into place with product and he had moisturised his face so much, it was as smooth as a baby's bottom. Sir had appreciated his presence, and knowing how much Morton took pride in his appearance, presented him with a very handsome comb and cufflinks.

Digby climbed onto the stage, his chest swelled out with pride. Never in his life had he had such an important role to play. Now everyone could see what a highly intelligent black Labrador he was. He stood straight and tall ,his coat sleek and black. He could not believe his eyes when Sir presented him with not only a Naval Captain's white hat, but a white naval jacket as well, with gold epaulettes and gold buttons with anchors on them. Sir said he was to be chief captain in future, as he had steered the boat so well. Digby was as proud as punch. Not only had he done something very special, he had also acquired a whole new group of wonderful friends.

His twin, Monty couldn't really see what all the fuss was about, although he could not help but being pleased for his brother. Where there was good food to be had, Monty always loved to be there. That was his purpose in life: to be a gourmand.

Finally, Horton rose onto the stage accompanied by whistling, cheering and much clapping from friends and locals. Wearing his best red shorts, long sleeved red silk shirt, red and white spotted dicky bow, and a red velevet waistcoat, he looked very handsome, even though his hair would not stay flat and he had funny ears, and his eyes were too bulgy and his hands and feet were out of proportion to the rest of his body.

Sir produced a gold Acme Thunderer whistle and handed it to Horton saying: "Had it not been for Horton's quick thinking and attention to detail, I might still be in the canal. I could have drowned! Through his leadership, advising these others "and he pointed at Ernie, Morton and Digby, "...what to do, I was saved from drowning. I know your much-loved whistle was lost in the canal that day, so I hope you will accept this with my heartfelt thanks!"

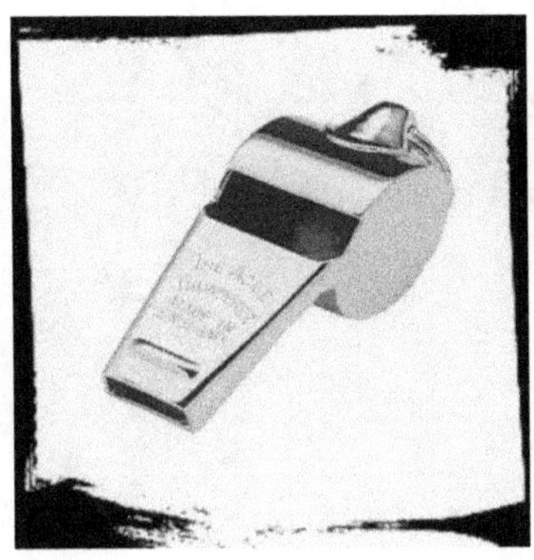

But not only were they amazed and delighted by their gifts, the biggest and best surprise was yet to come. Sir, Milady,Mr and Mrs Keeper led the party towards the carpark.

There, to the right of the entrance, on a patch of grass next to a straggly bush and under a large overhanging tree, was a wooden carving of two magnificent boxing hares. The plaque at the base was inscribed with the words 'Horton and Morton. The two BFF's whose quick thinking saved the life of Sir Thomas Bunglebury.'

Horton was so proud! He felt he had grown taller that day!

And then they all partied!

Part 2

Thieves!

SHhhh...........

Tiptoeing over the great lawn, the three intrepid masked Zorros, aided by a noiseless black Labrador, deposited their paraphernalia under a large spreading tree. A shaft of light suddenly beamed out of the front door. They all threw themselves flat on the dark grass.........

Chapter 1

The Alert

"Thieves! Thieves!"

Mrs. Keeper burst breathlessly into the sitting room where Sir and Milady were taking their morning cup of tea. Sir leapt up, alarmed, spilling hot tea down his trousers.

"Where, Mrs Keeper? I'll get my gun!"

"Not here, Sir. Out and about. In the village!"

Sir sat down, somewhat relieved, mopping his wet, tea stained trousers with his handkerchief. He had no wish to get the gun which was kept for security under lock and key in an old cabinet: he didn't even know when it had last been used or where the ammunition was kept.

Mrs. Keeper went on to explain that Mrs. Newhouse, who brought her eggs every day, had heard about a number of thefts around the village from Mrs Tibbles, owner of Bunbury Village grocery store.

The Tweets, who had been listening into the conservation as usual, had been thrown into a flummox at the sound of the word THIEVES.

The Tweets were garrulous, gossip mongers who had a hotline from The Hall and could listen into any conversation from below. They weren't really spying; they were just nosey and wanted to be the first to know if anything important was afoot.

Their system was quite ingenious. The listen-in-er sat at the edge of a drainpipe attached to The Hall by a series of hooks which secured it. Where there are screws there are holes, and these small holes allowed sound from The Hall to travel up and down the drainpipe. So The Tweet at the top could hear everything that was said inside. If it was really, really important there was room for two Tweets to listen in.

So when the word THIEVES was mentioned, the telephone wire had started bouncing up and down as messages were passed along. The Tweets bounced and balanced as it swayed back and forth, and the wire had become a balancing act as Tweets flew to and fro from the listening post. Usually, if the chat below wasn't too important, from the ground it looked just like a queue at a busy supermarket, each Tweet taking his turn. When The Tweet at the end completed his turn, the next Tweet in line would take his place and he would return to the other end of the queue. The difference was that there was no attempt at queue jumping and The Tweets were chattering amongst themselves all the time.

An observer of their antics could almost believe The Tweets were spies on important missions for MI6, except, of course, that they were very noisy and garrulous. It was easy to alert the attention of an observer that something was afoot.

Very important news would be passed on by The Tweets to the next port of call, The Robinettes, who would carry messages further afield, usually to Horton.

Horton had become a hero after saving Sir from drowning in the Canal. He had become a welcome visitor to The Hall: Sir and Milady enjoyed discussions with him; Mrs. Keeper loved the attention and help he gave her in the kitchen; Mr. Keeper told him what was happening around the estate; and Digby had become a firm friend. Horton had always been an ideas person, and he could always come up with an 'I Was thinking…'

proposition. There was always much to think about and do up at The Hall.

The Robinettes, as second line of defence from The Tweets, were of great importance as they acted as filters, sorting out the 'Need To Know' stuff from the 'Oh, that's Just Gossip ' stuff. They were the code-breakers: we need to pass this on to Horton; or this is just chaff and we can bin it. Pretty clever, really!

The very fact that the telephone wire was swaying violently backwards and forwards as well as bouncing up and down meant that there were very important things being talked about inside. Fortunately, there were no passers by in the vicinity, who would realise the importance of what was being discussed.

Mrs. Keeper's cry of "Thieves" had alerted and frightened The Tweets, who listened anxiously as

Mrs. Keeper explained to Sir and Milady that she had just heard that there had been a spate of robberies nearby.

" That's not good." said a worried Sir, rubbing his forehead. "We could be a target. We've lots of old paintings of my ancestors by Old Masters which are very valuable, as well as priceless collections which have been accumulated over centuries."

These valuables included miniatures painted by Levina Teerlinc. She was a Flemish member of The Queen's bedchamber who had painted many miniatures for Queen Elizabeth the First. They had been given to the first Sir Thomas Bunglebury, the first owner of The Hall. He had been pardoned for his Acts of Piracy and allowed to keep his illicit gains, in return for providing his pirate ship and extensive sea-faring knowledge to fight for The Queen against the forthcoming Spanish invasion. The fluke canon ball descending on the arsenal of the Spanish Admiral of the Fleet had turned the tide of the Spanish/English War and Sir Thomas had become one of the Queen's favourites and confidante.

 Amongst the booty he had accumulated were gold, jewels, silks, spices and other valuable plate seized from Spanish galleons. It might have been difficult for these riches and The Hall and its lands to have been kept in Sir's family over the centuries, for since then, his ancestors had swapped sides and allegiances whenever necessary to keep in the favour of Kings and Queens who had come to the throne. The estate had grown and flourished, even when taxes and Death Duties had to be paid, and gambling debts (such as horse racing or bets on very stupid things like whose snail would be first over a line , or who would blink first in a staring match) caused very large amounts of cash to be lost.

There was a lot of valuable items in The Hall, so Sir was naturally very worried.

The Tweets were in a quandary. "What to do? What to do?"

Some flew frantically to The Robinettes. "This is bad!"

Only one person they could think of would be able to help. He would know how to keep The Hall safe.

Chapter Two

The List

The news was so important, so urgent that even a Tweet flew with The Robinettes.

It seemed to take forever to get there, but at last they found Horton in his red shorts and red t-shirt, stretched out on his red deckchair in his carefully pruned, neatly cut lawn and red and white flower filled bordered garden, eating a pink strawberry coned ice cream with a chocolate flake.

"What's the panic?" Horton asked in a calm, casual voice.

 "Robbers, burglars, thieves! They're going to steal from The Hall! Help! What can you do?"

Horton had been relaxing in his neat and tidy garden. He had worked hard all morning; clearing up, repairing broken fences, mowing the lawn, pruning the hedge and doing some weeding. He had been very busy and now he was having his downtime, enjoying the sunny weather, looking at white fluffy clouds turning into shapes of elephants, dragons, or mushrooms in the bright blue sky. He was certainly not in an 'I Was Thinking' mood.

Now, suddenly, here was a crisis. Time to start thinking.

Quickly Horton leapt up from his deckchair, dropping the remains of his ice cream on the floor. "Start thinking! Start thinking!" his mind screamed at him.

The Tweet and the Robinettes hopped agitatedly, waiting for a response. They did not want the whole world to know about this. This was VERY IMPORANT! Walls have ears and anything they said could easily be passed on to these horrible brigands. So whatever needed to be done had to be carried out secretly and very, very quietly. The Tweets and The Robinettes had to keep very, very calm. No more frantic activity which might alert others. That was the first thing Horton now thought.

Next he really had to put on his 'I Was Thinking' hat. He didn't actually have a hat because of his loppy ear, but he had been wearing his red bandanna with white spots because he'd been working very hard and it prevented sweat running down into his eyes and also stopped him from getting sunburnt. That would have to do.He scratched his head, twisted his whiskers, paced up and down and scratched his head again.

The Tweet and The Robinettes stood looking at him, anxiously waiting.

"Hmm! I was thinking there are a few ways we could foil these robbers and make life very uncomfortable for them" Horton announced.

So Horton and The Robinettes huddled round together, while The Tweet flew back to the line to tell the rest of them that Horton had taken charge and had been thinking and the first thing they all needed to do was KEEP VERY CALM and do nothing untoward (that is, anything different from what they usually do).

Horton decided that the first thing he needed to do was to make a list.

Nothing could ever be done without A LIST. It made sure you didn't forget anything. There is nothing worse than starting to do something and in the middle to find out you haven't got the right tools, or you'd forgotten the plan of how to do it when you got to a complicated bit. So The LIST is vital.To write a LIST you need pen and paper, so the initial task was to find those. This is always more difficult than you would expect; paper has always something written on it and pens have always run out of ink when you need them.Finally they were ready, so The Robinettes and Horton huddled round again to make THE LIST,

It started:

LIST TO FOIL THE ROBBERS

1. *Marbles*
2. *Black paint*
3. *Spade*
4. *Tarpaulin*
5. *Some artificial grass*
6. *Wire*
7. *Two bicycle torches*
8. *Batteries*
9. *Soldering kit*
10. *Large tyre*
11. *Rope*

"I think that's all we need! Can you take this note to Morton and explain the situation, please? Be sure to tell him no-one else must know. Can he check the list and see if he already has some of the things in his back garden? Do not breathe a word of this to any other soul!" Horton whispered to the Robinettes as they flew off instantly. "I will follow shortly."

Not only did Horton not want any burglars to know that they were aware of their activity in the neighbourhood, but he also did not want Mr. Keeper to know that he was involved in a scheme. Although Mr. Keeper knew everything and could solve many problems, Horton realised that if Mr. Keeper got wind of his scheme, he would probably call it hare-brained and that it would never work and typical of 'I Was Thinking ' Horton, who should know better. Definitely better to keep the formidable Mr. Keeper and everyone else in the dark.

Horton cleared out his Just-In-Case rucksack, and then put in screwdrivers, hammer, nuts and bolts, nails and screws, spanners, pliers and wire cutters. Morton usually kept most of these in his Everything In It blue rucksack, but this time Horton thought they might need two lots of everything. He also kept his First Aid Kit, in case they needed plasters and antiseptic cleaning wipes. Better to be prepared in case you hammered your thumb, or pierced a finger with a nail.

 Everyone was so used to seeing Horton go round with his red Just-In-Case rucksack slung over one shoulder, they wouldn't take a second glance at him going over to Morton's house.

Horton had sent the list to Morton in advance, so that he could start looking for things they would need.

Morton's garden was like his house, very untidy. It was full of stuff which he thought might be really useful one day. Nobody was sure – useful for what? But he did have bits of wood of different shapes and sizes, old bicycles, plastic boxes containing nuts, bolts, screws, old taps, tape measures, and even ladders. So even if people weren't sure what Morton's bits and pieces were useful for, they still went round to see if Morton had it before they went to the Do It Yourself shop, and could save themselves quite a lot of money.

Morton took the list and started searching through his garden. He ticked off the list as he found things and pulled them out to the front of his back garden

.

"What an extraordinary list" he thought to himself, "But there must be method in Horton's madness!"

Black paint.

Spade.

Artificial grass. (Morton even had some of that, picked up after the completion of the new village football pitch).

Wire.

Two bicycle lights, which he had retrieved from a couple of broken bicycles .

Batteries.

Large tyre, which he thought might be useful as a swing one day .

Rope. which could come in handy to make the large tyre into a swing.

So the only two things he didn't have were marbles and a soldering kit.

On his way over to Morton's house in Dingley Dell, Horton made a slight detour via Pinkie's home. He shouted up to her sitting on a branch at the top of a tree, "Pinkie, I need your help, please!"   She bounded down.

"I wondered if you'd be able to get three Zorro outfits. We're having a fancy dress party tomorrow, and of course you are invited too." Horton explained.

Pinkie didn't think there was anything extraordinary in this. She loved parties, especially dressing up ones, and she was the custodian of all the costumes in the area. Her parents had been disappointed she had not become a detective , especially as they had named her Pinkerton after that famous detective agency, but she had started an agency of some sort . A Fancy Dress Agency! She could get her hands on anything which was required, and everything was stored in a secret huge, camouflaged hollow   under a large old broken tree in the woods .

"Come with me," she replied as Horton followed her to her secret stash of costumes. She pulled out three black Zorro outfits as Horton said "See you tomorrow late afternoon at my house. Thanks for these!"

 Stuffing the outfits into the front of his Just In Case rucksack, he resumed his path to Morton's home.

Chapter Three

Assembling the Team

When Horton arrived, he and Morton discussed his 'I Was Thinking' plan, and decided that there was one more person needed to put the plan into action. The Robinettes flew off again with strict instructions to not tell a soul and to only speak to their friend Hardip.

Immediately he heard the message, Hardip grabbed three black hats from his collection, locked the door of Hatter's House, sat astride his orange bike, pulled on his orange helmet and pedalled for all his worth to Morton's house in Dingley Dell.

Hardip was extremely clever. He knew that if you had to change a fuse, mend a plug or change a lightbulb you HAD to turn off the electricity. He knew that if you wanted to change a tap or de-gunge a U-bend you HAD to turn off the water.

Hardip was really excellent at that sort of technical stuff, and in a crisis where you needed someone to make certain that everything would go right, Hardip was that person.

His home, Hatter's House had originally been called Hatter's Cottage, but Hardip, as well as being very talented with electricity and electronics and plumbing and all that sort of work, was a very enthusiastic collector of HATS! As his collection grew, so did his house.

Hardip could not help himself. He had replica Elizabethan hats with magnificent feathers and plumes; he had Georgian wigs of all shapes and sizes; he had top hats, trilbies, flat caps, baseball caps, deer stalkers, vintage motoring hats, pork pie hats. And not just hats for men, but ladies' hats as well. Lace caps, wigs, bonnets, Edwardian hats; hats right up to the latest fashions which might be worn at the Ascot Races or weddings. As his compulsion to acquire hats grew, so did Hatter's Cottage which had to be extended and adapted to accommodate them all.

Hardip arrived huffing and puffing from the exertion of pedalling his bicycle so hard.

"What's the problem?" he puffed as he thrust the three black hats into Horton's hands.

 Horton explained the situation, adding "If you don't mind, Hardip, we could do with your expertise!"

Naturally, Hardip was only too willing to help, and also said he had a soldering kit and a marble game with hundreds of marbles back at his house, and he would go and get them straight away. He pedalled his way back to Hatter's House on his orange bicycle as fast as his little legs could go.

Had anyone looked in through his window, they would have been surprised to see hats flying everywhere as Hardip searched for the illusory marble game. Eventually Hardip discovered it at the bottom of a battered old trunk. He grabbed hold of it and the soldering iron and raced back to Dingley Dell.

No-one would have batted an eyelid as the three pals went into Morton's back garden as this wasn't an unusual occurrence.

Now they could start putting Horton's ingenious plan into action.

At this stage, they realised that there was one more accomplice they needed and that was Digby, one of Sir's black Labradors, who had become another of their trusted friends. He was to be instrumental in getting them access to the grounds without anyone else realising.

Digby was one of identical twin, completely black Labradors belonging to Sir. The only feature that set them apart was Digby sometimes wore a red collar and Monty had a blue one. To all intents and purposes they appeared identical: they both learned quickly and did as they were told. Digby had become renown for being the sailor who had steered the little electric boat to safety, yet he and Monty were indistinguishable from each other unless they wore their coloured collars. When they were not wearing them, Digby could sneak off and do his own thing. Only then could Digby blame his misdemeanours on Monty, and Monty being very acquiescent and a bit lazy, never disputed them. Monty had a penchant for food and didn't like being too far from The Hall's kitchen. At the moment, he and Digby looked the same, but in the future that might change!

Digby received his message from The Robinettes and was very excited to be playing such an important part in the proceedings. He prepared himself by giving Monty extra helpings of dinner and large portions of Mrs. Keeper's delicious chocolate cake, which he had snaffled from the kitchen. He thought, correctly, that if Monty was very full, he would sleep soundlessly through the night without stirring.

Preparation was a key element of the plan, and they needed to make sure everything would work before they noiselessly entered the grounds of The Hall at nightfall.

Horton, Morton and Hardip painted the marbles black; measured and cut out circles of tarpaulin and artificial grass; soldered blackened wire to the Bicycle lamps which now lit up at a touch; and, having practiced using one of Mr. Keeper's knots, knew how to attach the length of blackened rope to the large tyre. Finally they had to adjust two of the black hats, one of which had to fit over the one loppy and one straight uppy ear of Horton, and the two tall upright ears of Morton. Fortunately, although spiky, Hardip's head was fairly flat so the third black hat needed no alteration.

Time had slipped past, and now they were ready. All that could be done had been tried out before their cunning plan was put into action .

The pals decided to have a quick tea of corned beef and cucumber sandwiches washed down with glasses of orange squash. It could be a long night and they weren't sure when they would finish and have a chance to eat their next meal.

Chapter Four

Setting the Trap

Night fell.

It was time to go.

Fortunately it was a moonless and cloudy night when the three, all dressed in their black Zorro costumes with their black hats, quietly slipped out of Morton's back garden. They were laden with all the paraphernalia they required for Horton's 'I Was Thinking; Foil the Robbers' plan.

The large tyre was the most cumbersome thing they had to carry. The tarpaulin and the artificial grass were rolled up and Morton carried these in his blue Everything In It rucksack. Horton's red Just In Case rucksack bulged, laden with marbles packed in cotton wool to prevent them from making a noise. It also held the bicycle lamps, lengths of wire, and, of course, the inevitable First

Aid Kit. Better to be safe than sorry. Horton and Morton struggled along carrying the tyre between them. Hardip trudged along behind with the rope

slung over his shoulders: the coil was almost as big as himself.

Silently they hurried along the grass verge, so their feet were noiseless on the road and the gravelled path leading to The Hall.

Monty was so gorged from the delicious food Digby very kindly kept offering him, he fell asleep in front of the fireplace. He only half raised an eyelid as Digby silently padded out, and remained fast asleep during the whole night. Digby silently strode down to the entrance to the grounds to let them in. Digby could hardly see them, but he knew it was them because of his acute sense of smell.

"Now to get this show on the road!" whispered Horton.

He instructed Digby to dig, with Morton's help, five deep circular holes at regular intervals across the grass. While they did this. Horton and Hardip rigged up the blackened wire to the two bicycle lamps, each of which was placed at an angle of forty five degrees about two metres high, and camouflaged in a tree facing The Hall. Then they attached the rope and the tyre to an overhanging branch. This was a particularly difficult task. Hardip, as the shortest of the crew, had the job of steadying the tyre as Horton heaved on the rope as he had finally managed to throw the end of it over the unbending branch.

They were all wearing masks as part of their Zorro outfits as they also hoped to be incognito just in case anyone saw them, which was highly unlikely. The only problem was that Hardip's mask kept slipping over his spectacles and he had to keep letting go of the tyre with one hand to push the mask up, otherwise he couldn't see what he was doing. Horton hauled the tyre up vigorously labouring under the its weight, Hardip steadying it for as long as he possibly could. Finally, it was in the right place and the last job was to put the trip wires in place across the lawn, so that they were invisible from The Hall or the entrance to the grounds.

By this time, Digby and Morton had finished digging the deep circular holes.

Sir opened the front door and light flooded out in a narrow beam.

The team held their breaths and threw themselves down flat on the pitch black lawn.

Would Sir spot anything untoward on this uninviting , moonless and starless night?

He looked upwards, reflected disappointedly there were no constellations to be seen this night. Sir stepped back into The Hall. The door closed. The beam of light disappeared. The team silently congratulated themselves on their invisibility, and also heaved sighs of relief that they had not yet put the blackened marbles in place.

Now the tarpaulin needed to be stretched seamlessly over the five deep, circular holes and finally the artificial grass was placed carefully on top, ensuring there were no lumps or bumps in it. Satisfied with their work, the very last task was to put the marbles in place.

This was the most difficult part of their mission as they had to work so noiselessly laying the marbles down just in front of doors and windows. At last, their work completed, the four vanished into the night.

"Well done, everyone," congratulated Horton. "Now time for a sleep!"

Chapter Five

The Plan in Action

Horton awoke to loud yells, and lots of shouting and shrieking. He had not gone home to his bed as he wanted to be close by, and had curled himself up on a bed of leaves under a bush.

It was that crepuscular time of day, just between night and dawn. The sky was growing lighter but was still a dark grey colour, no sign of the sun.

At this moment, The Tweets were very proud of themselves because, for the first time ever, they had managed to curb their gossiping and not given the plan away. Now they flew and swooped doing loop the loops and acrobatic manoeuvres in the air and calling to each other vociferously.

Horton looked over to where they were performing. He saw two bespectacled men with their heads just peeping out of the ground. One had a large tyre around his neck, their faces were bright red from anger and embarrassment and were spot lit from the two shining bicycle lamps.

"It worked. It really worked!" Horton congratulated himself, and then found he was also being congratulated by his three friends Morton, Hardip and Digby who had just arrived on the scene with The Robinettes circling above them.

At the first howl of anger and anguish from the thieves when they had found themselves trapped, the police had been alerted by the Robinettes.

They arrived in their police vans, blue lights flashing and sirens blaring. They leapt out of their vans blowing their shrill police whistles.

"What's all this, then?" a policeman enquired, looking at the trapped men.

"Horton's caught the thieves!" The Robinettes responded.

"No!" exclaimed Horton."WE'VE caught the thieves! After all, it was a joint effort!"

"What a clever ruse; whoever thought of this trap must be a genius!"

 Horton felt his chest swelling with pride.

Getting the two bespectacled, booted and suited, and now very dirty men out of the deep, muddy holes was proving to be extremely difficult.

In the dark night, just before dawn, the immaculately dressed men clutching their notepads, were completely unaware of anything unusual in the grounds. They had entered silently, and tripped over the blackened wire which immediately lit up the two bicycle lamps.

In their surprise, they stumbled onto the artificial grass which, with the tarpaulin underneath, gave way and they dropped unexpectedly into the large, deep circular holes. One of the men set off another wire attached to the large tyre hanging by a rope in the overhanging tree. This was an insurance to definitely prevent escape: if the other thief managed to struggle free, the one with a tyre around his neck certainly wouldn't be able to.

The police grasped and pulled, pulled and grasped as if it was a tug of war match, and eventually the two thieves were hoisted from the slurpy muddy holes with a loud PLOP!

With much consternation, the two irate men were manhandled into the police van, both protesting their innocence, and were driven back to the police station at high speed. Once again the blue lights flashed and the sirens blared. Villagers stopped and stared at the commotion as they began to make their way to work.

What on earth had been going on as they had slept dreamlessly through the night?

The tyre was removed as evidence.

In all the commotion, the only victims at The Hall were Sir's other black Labrador, Monty, and Sir himself.

Sir, woken by the extraordinary cacophony outside, had rushed downstairs in his striped Wynciette pyjamas and opened the front door.

Fortunately he did not have time to step outside as Monty flew past him, barking ferociously to show what an excellent guard dog he was! As his feet hit the marbles, he skidded, his feet splayed wide, and, like a champion skater, he spun round. With a little yelp, he performed an amazing somersault and backflip. He did not land upright, alas, and could be seen flat on his back. his legs flailing around in the air, whining piteously as he hit his head on the doorpost as he landed. Poor Monty!

Sir carefully picked his way out onto the lawn in his pyjamas.

What on earth was going on?

He wandered down onto the grass trying to get a closer look at the paraphernalia scattered on the ground. As he strode forward, his slippered feet gave way below him, as he rapidly descended into one of the holes which had not yet been uncovered.

Sir was stuck! The more he tried to free himself, the more stuck he became; and the dirtier and muddier he looked.

Milady did her best, but the more she pulled, the more fixed Sir became.

Finally, it was the Fire Service who came to his rescue, and using ropes and brute strength, they hefted him from the deep hole, laughing at the ridiculously filthy figure in his muddy blue striped Wynciette pyjamas and dirty bare feet, his slippers having fallen to the bottom of the hole.

"You need a soothing hot bath, before you do anything else!" said Milady comfortingly, hiding a smile at Sir's ridiculous figure.

Following her very sheepishly, Sir returned into The Hall, before going down to the police station, to clean up and enjoy a warming cup of sweet tea with some of Mrs. Keeper's delicious ginger biscuits.

Meanwhile, three figures in Zorro costumes could be seen cavorting across the lawn.

While Digby collected together the apparatus they had used, Horton, Morton, and Hardip produced imaginary swords from their outfits and began to playfence. Firstly Morton and Hardip had pretend sword fights shouting "I'm Zorro!" at each other until Hardip fell to the ground having been lightly jabbed by Morton's sword .There he remained, pretending to be lifeless while Horton, flailing his imaginary sword in the air, parried and thrust his sword at Morton , both of them shouting "I'm Zorro!" in turn . Finally , with a flourish from Horton, Morton dropped to his knees and fell on his back clutching his chest . Horton raised his foot and placed it lightly on Morton's chest. "I am Zorro!" and he held his hand high as if brandishing his imaginary powerful sword. At this all three and Digby rolled around on the ground, splitting their sides with laughter.

Following their interrogation at the police station in the presence of Sir, it transpired that the two men weren't thieves at all, even though they had acted like them in attempting to gain access to the grounds. They had been sent by the bank to get details of The Hall.

Sir was what was known as 'Property rich, cash poor'. That meant that although he was the possessor of this fine Elizabethan mansion, he didn't really have enough ready money to pay for all the things that needed doing to maintain it and keep it in good order. The bank was preparing to take it over.

Horton was still regarded as a hero for catching them, as it had alerted Sir to the fact that he really did need to raise some money for various alterations and general upkeep of The Hall, something he did not want to do by selling off any of the precious heirlooms and antiques which were being preserved for posterity.

However, this meant that there must be some robbers still at large, so Mr. Keeper said "It's up to me to sort this out. If Horton had told me his plan," he grumbled," I would have said it was really a hare-brained scheme, even though it did work. Just look at the state of that lawn! It has come to my notice, though, that Hardip is a very clever person and I would like him to help me rig up burglar alarms, CCTV and other anti-theft devices around The Hall. As a precaution, in case the real thieves are still at large."

Hardip was thrilled his handiwork had been approved of, and, of course, was delighted to be of help.

So the day ended with complete satisfaction all round, and Mrs. Keeper providing large mugs of delicious hot chocolate and plates of warm, freshly baked gooey flapjacks and Horton's favourite chocolate biscuits.

And Monty, feeling very sorry for himself, lying at Mrs. Keeper's feet, head bandaged, being given tasty titbits and Mrs. Keeper stroking him gently saying "There! There!"

Chapter Six

More Thieves

"Thieves! Thieves!" shrieked Mrs. Keeper, when she returned to the kitchen, having only left it for a few minutes to use the bathroom.

Milady came running in from the sitting room. Her quick eyes scanned the kitchen. The kettle, the toaster, food processor, coffee maker, the expensive set of Sabatier knives; everything seemed to be in place.

She looked quizzically at Mrs. Keeper.

 "My wicker basket," cried Mrs. Keeper. "It's gone!"

Mrs. Keeper had spent the morning busily making cakes for the village Cake Fair that afternoon. She had baked a chocolate cake decorated with Morello cherries and chocolate grenache; a Lemon Drizzle cake topped with a light lemon fondant icing; carrot cake with mascarpone top decorated with tiny orange coloured marzipan carrots, fabulicious fairy cakes, butterfly cakes and lots of different types of scones.These she had all carefully placed in the wicker basket to be taken into the village where Mary Berry was to be the judge of the annual cake baking competition at the Village Memorial Hall.

But now the wicker basket had vanished, the kitchen door left ajar, and no sign of the perpetrator of this dreadful crime.

Mr. Keeper came bursting in. "Thieves! Let me at them!"

He was distraught.

He and Hardip had not yet had time to install the CCTV and burglar alarms, and the thought that perhaps someone had run off with some of the priceless valuables from The Hall had really alarmed him. In fact, he let out a sigh of relief when he realised it was ONLY Mrs. Keeper's wicker basket of cakes that had been taken. He gave Mrs. Keeper a hug and a kiss though, as he knew how important these cakes were to her.

Had they all looked outside straight away, they would have seen a black Labrador bounding down the path, swinging a wicker basket to and fro.

Where was he off to?

5, Willow Wood Cottages of course!

Now accompanied by The Tweets and The Robinettes, it was party time for the heroes.

Pinkie arrived dressed as Red Riding Hood, and there they all were Horton, Morton, Hardip,(all dressed, of course, as Zorro) Digby (now wearing his naval captain's hat) singing and laughing, reminiscing about the men in the holes, and scoffing the delicious cakes until they were so full they came to a standstill.

The Robinettes had informed Ernestine and Corwen of the goings on at The Hall. Not wanting to miss out on congratulating Horton and his three clever accomplices,they had made their way down to 5, Willow Wood Cottages. They knew that where there was an excuse, the friends would always be ready to party.

Mrs. Keeper, arriving back empty handed at the end of the day and devoid of any prizes she might have won from the Cake Fair, was astonished to see before her, on the kitchen table, the large, empty wicker basket.

Lying on the sheepskin rug in front of a blazing fire were two black Labradors, one with a red collar, the other with a blue one. The blue collared Labrador with head bandage removed, had a mouth covered in incriminating cake crumbs. "Monty, you naughty dog!" she yelled. He was really in the doghouse now.

Digby, the crafty fellow, had got away with running off with the cakes. He did have a pang of conscience and decided he would have to give Monty the last piece of chocolate cake. Oh dear!

Chapter Seven

Foxy

Pinkie had thoroughly enjoyed herself at Horton's party.

It was wonderful to escape from the crowded surroundings of her home where she was surrounded by fighting, smelly and argumentative brothers. She always loved dressing up and she had a secret stash of dressing up clothes hidden in a camouflaged hollow under an enormous old tree in Dingley Dell.

Today, not only did she have her brothers to contend with, but Great Aunt Wilhelmina had also come to stay.

Even at bedtime, she could have no peace because she had to share her bed with her elderly great aunt.

Great Aunt Wilhelmina was getting on in years and had old-fashioned ideas. She was always telling Pinkie how to do things, how to behave and it seemed to Pinkie that she criticised only her and not her ragamuffin brothers. She also smelt of lavender water, which really was an old person's smell, and Pinkie wanted to smell young and fresh.

Great Aunt Wilhelmina had decided to stay until she had enough nuts and acorns to see her through the winter, as she did not want to venture out if the weather became too bad and cold. The family had offered to help collect them. Even though the boys had plenty of scraps and arguments, their hearts were in the right place and they were always generous, kind and helpful.

Perhaps Great Aunt Wilhelmina would not overstay her welcome.

Pinkie hoped she wouldn't.

Today, the day after the party, Pinkie had escaped once more to Horton's house when there was a knock at his door.

Mrs. Newhouse had arrived at Horton's cottage with a delivery of eggs. Mrs. Newhouse was very handsome, dressed in a rich black feathery cape and wearing an emerald green hat.

" I'm really sorry, Horton," she explained. "I've only got two eggs for you, today."

She carried on to say that when she had gone to collect the eggs from The Hen Hut, the fence had been cut. There was a large hole, and there were footprints leading up to the coop. There weren't the usual number of eggs for her to collect, and after her deliveries to Mrs. Tibbles at The Grocery Store and Mrs. Keeper at The Hall, she only had two eggs to offer to Horton instead of the usual two dozen.

"I think I've been robbed," she moaned to Horton and Pinkie.

Mrs. Newhouse had been the person who had alerted Mrs. Keeper to the fact that there were thieves in Bunbury. She had moaned to her as well when she had made her delivery to The Hall, saying she was upset that today there were not enough eggs for all her customers, and she hoped Horton would not be too upset,as he was her last delivery of the day.

Of course, Mrs. Keeper had immediately alerted Milady, and by the time Horton was going to tell Mr. Keeper, as he had promised to share any suspicious activity with him straight away, Mr. Keeper already knew about the theft of the eggs.

Mr. Keeper would know what to do, and he would certainly repair The Hen Hut for Mrs. Newhouse as well as examining the footprints.

Horton had promised Pinkie an omelette for lunch so gratefully accepting Mrs. Newhouse's proffering of only two eggs, he decided he would let Mr. Keeper know later.

Two eggs would make a measly small omelette, so telling Pinkie to wait a moment, he rushed off to buy more eggs from Mrs. Tibble's shop.

On his way he passed an elderly lady struggling with a very large suitcase.

 A few minutes later, he returned from the shop with his eggs and saw the same elderly lady lying face down on the pavement, the suitcase no longer with her.

He looked up and down the street and saw a trail of nuts and acorns, and a brown coloured furry back scurrying down the street dragging the large open suitcase.

Helping her to her feet, Great Aunt Wilhelmina explained. "It was time for me to leave! They were getting on my nerves with their fighting and arguing. They had been fantastic helping fill my larder for winter, but I knew it was time to go. And now this! Someone has stolen my case and all my preserves for the winter. I don't think I could cope with staying longer. What shall I do?" she wailed.

Checking she was not badly injured, Horton helped her into The Bunglebury Arms where she sat down with a cup of strong tea and some shortbread biscuits to settle her nerves. Then he returned to follow the trail of nuts and acorns.

The Robinettes had been accompanying Horton on his shopping trip. They were alarmed witnessing the scene, but Horton told them to remain calm: he needed The Robinettes to take a message back to Pinkie that he was sorry he would be delayed. "Don't mention the attack on Great Aunt

Willhelmina as Pinkie will be distraught," he advised them. "And I don't want her to come here as I think I am going to be quite busy for a while."

Just as he thought, the trail led to a hole in the ground in Dingley Dell. He hoped his BFF Morton would be at home, as now he knew where the thief's lair was, he was sure Morton would assist him.

A brown coloured furry back; the door in the tree leading to a a hole in the ground: there was only one person who could be the robber. Quickly and quietly the two pals made their way from Morton's house to the tree carrying a large net, which they had commandeered from Morton's back garden.

As they got closer, they knew the perpetrator was still inside.

The delicious smell of eggs and the spitting sound of frying wafted its way towards the two friends.

They could also see the freshly made trail of nuts and acorns leading up to and into the entrance.

Silently they split up, one sentry-like on each side of the hole, spreading the net over the entrance. It wasn't long before the sound of cutlery scraping on a plate and the slurping noise finished. There was a pitter-patter of things being dropped into a bag; they assumed it was the contraband being put away.

Horton and Morton hoped it wouldn't be long before the thief would leave his lair, and, sure enough, out he came brazenly and without a care in e world. Straight into the trap he walked.

Horton and Morton were ready to tighten the net around him so that when he wriggled, the net became even tighter.

"Foxy! You thief!" they cried . "How could you? Don't you realise how much trouble and upset you have caused?"

Completely entangled in the net, Horton and Morton marched Foxy straight down to the police station. The police were issued with a warrant and immediately went to search Foxy's lair.

Inside his den they retrieved: two pairs of soft leather gloves; a silk gentleman's scarf and a cashmere scarf; two walking canes embossed and decorated with silver tops; three walking sticks with beautifully carved handles in the shape of ducks and elephants; and a man's drinking flask of aquamarine colour with a crest engraved on it.

Foxy obviously had expensive tastes, but was not prepared to work to achieve them.

There was also a pile of cracked eggshells thrown down on the kitchen floor and a dirty frying pan.

Foxy was subsequently charged with robbery having been caught red handed. "The local robber has been apprehended and charged with burglary", it was announced by the local radio station.

The News Programme ran the story and invited Horton and Morton to share their story with the listeners.

Going in front of the Magistrate, Foxy's knees were knocking and his teeth chattered loudly. He was feeling very contrite as he stood in the dock. He had remembered from where he had stolen his ill gotten gains and made a list so the police could return the articles to their rightful owners.

There was no way he was going to be allowed to walk out from the court scot-free, even though his victims had been reunited with their stolen belongings, and he paid Mrs. Newhouse compensation for the stolen eggs, which had been such a delicious feast.

Taking his remorse for his actions into consideration, Foxy was sentenced to do a year's community service after firstly picking up enough nuts and acorns to fill Great Aunt Wilhelmina's suitcase and stockpile dumps for other elderly folk to use if they so required.

Everyone was so relieved. They didn't need to be jumpy and wary any more. They could look at each other without suspicion, and life could go back to normal.

Most importantly, Great Aunt Willehelmina had not sustained any physical injuries, and, furthermore, could return to her home knowing she had adequate supplies for the coming winter.

Pinkie was delighted she could have her own bed again and didn't need to share it . Her brothers could once again rough and tumble and argue as much as they liked.

The whole village came out to congratulate the hero and his associate. "Three cheers for Horton and his BFF Morton. Hip, Hip, Hooray!".

Bunbury Village and The Hall could return to some

sense of normality once more .

Part Three

Saving The Hall!

DRIP.......Drip.......Dripp..Drippp....d r i ppp!

Sir laboriously climbed the stairs up to the attic. He placed another two steel buckets under the new leaks which had appeared in the roof. The number of buckets now totalled seven in all.

He looked up at his leaky roof. "How many more buckets will we need?" he wondered. Suddenly, there was a loud crack as the floor gave way............

Chapter One

Foxy's Task

Mr. Keeper was appointed mentor to Foxy by the magistrate.

Foxy had been caught red handed by Horton, the village Hero, and his BFF, Morton.

Horton had followed the trail of acorns and nuts spilling out from the battered brown suitcase which had been viciously stolen from Pinkie's Great Aunt Willhelmina. It had led him to Foxy's lair, where the brigand had been cooking. Horton and Morton had caught him in the act of frying eggs which had been stolen from The Hen Hut, and had netted him so tightly that no escape was possible.

Following his apprehension, Foxy had been charged with the robbery of various items from the villagers and sentenced to a year's community service around the village instead of a custodial sentence. Mr. Keeper, as an upstanding member of the community, was appointed to oversee him.

Mr. Keeper had looked on from a distance while a contrite Foxy had stumbled through the woodlands collecting nuts and acorns to replace those stolen from Great Aunt Willhelmina. When he had gathered enough for her winter needs, Foxy had had to continue the task replenishing the stores for other elderly villagers. It was arduous, back breaking work and finally Mr. Keeper allowed an exhausted Foxy to return home.

Foxy handed the huge battered brown suitcase bulging with nuts and acorns to Great Aunt Willhelmina, who, always polite in any circumstances, thanked him profusely for his efforts. At this, Foxy felt a variety of different emotions: he was greatly ashamed of what he had done; he felt really sorry for people like Great Aunt

Willhelmina, who found it difficult to do things for themselves, because they were getting older; yet he felt proud of his efforts and found an element of satisfaction in being praised for the good work he had done. These were all new emotions to him; he particularly liked the praise because he had never been praised for anything before, only being told off for being naughty and not doing things correctly. It gave him a warm feeling inside to know he was being appreciated.

Mr. Keeper told Foxy as he left, to meet him by the kitchen door to The Hall at 8.30 a.m. sharp, the following day. He would then be taken to start work on his next task.

Mr. Keeper had been pondering over this next job for Foxy. He felt it needed to be worthwhile: something which, when completed, Foxy and the community would be really pleased about. He had thought long and hard, scratched his head a lot, pushed his spectacles up and down on his forehead, had come up with ideas and then dismissed them, and finally had arrived at a Very Good Idea.

There was an area of land which had lain abandoned for almost a century. It was always last of the jobs on Mr. Keeper's To Do list, and never reached anywhere near the top. The land was some distance from The Hall and Mr. Keeper only visited it on rare occasions. He would give Foxy the job of clearing it and restoring it to a place of natural beauty, instead of an eyesore. People in Bunbury could then use it as a place for leisure as The Hall's grounds were open to everyone local. This would be very hard work and would really prove to everyone in the village that Foxy was truly repentant and could change his ways.

The area he had in mind was at the edge of The Hall's estate; a cutting alongside a hill, now overgrown with undergrowth and brambles. In the past it had been accessed from the lake in front of The Hall by a canal, now in a great state of disrepair, or by taking a long route overland through rarely used footpaths and bridleways through The Hall's fields. Only the occasional brave rambler went into the area, and had to battle his way through thickets and thorns.

 Meeting Foxy at the kitchen door at the appointed time, Mr. Keeper led the way over stiles and through rusty kissing gates along an overgrown pathway alongside a stagnant stretch of water in the disused canal until, at last, he stopped and pointed upwards. Foxy's eyes followed the pointing finger. Steep hills on either side covered with thick woodland led to the top of a chalky rocky cliff with the occasional tree and shrub growing down it.

"That," motioned Mr. Keeper, "is the Abandoned Quarry! It's not been touched for over a century since the last of the limestone quarrymen finished working there. Once upon a time, it was a busy, bustling hive of activity as people used chalk and lime for building their houses. When bricks became popular, the need for this decreased and eventually there was no further requirement for the stuff and the quarry was eventually abandoned, along with the canal which we've just walked alongside. Your task, Foxy, is to clear it up!"

Foxy's heart sank and he groaned to himself. He had felt so pleased with himself, and now he was completely deflated at the enormity of this proposed task. He did want to do the right thing and to do his best, but was this asking too much of him? His jaw dropped.

"I will be around to give you advice, and will give you the tools to do the job," Mr. Keeper said. "And nobody expects you to finish tomorrow. It is a huge undertaking, but what is expected is that you will do your best. "

"I will try!" responded Foxy, thinking that the times when he could laze about and do whatever he pleased had gone forever. He also realised that even though it would be boring and mind numbingly dull, the consequences of him not doing the work would be worse.

Mr. Keeper, as his mentor, reminded him about moral responsibilities and the need to help people less fortunate than himself. Foxy felt very ashamed of himself, and felt even worse than when he was shaking in his shoes standing before the magistrate, listening to his dressing down and lecture before being sentenced. Mr. Keeper, fair but firm, was a very formidable man, and his reputation for being a bit of a stickler was well known.

" What repercussions there will be if I don't commit myself to this task?" Foxy remonstrated with himself.

"I will give you safety instructions on how to use any tools you might need, and I will also demonstrate how to prune and coppice bushes and trees. You may also need to do some abseiling down the quarry face, so before you start, we will have a practice."

Mr. Keeper explained everything in detail and Foxy practised with the different tools, learnt how to put on and use safety equipment correctly and the different methods of clearing and cutting back the growth. Practice sessions took place nearer The Hall, and finally the abseiling had to be practised at the quarry.

Poor Foxy shook with fear as he took his first step over the cliff edge. He felt abandoned in mid-air, but Mr. Keeper gently advised him what to do and in no time, Foxy was thoroughly enjoying this new skill. Satisfied that Foxy was capable of following procedures and knew what to do. Mr. Keeper now felt they should take all necessary equipment to The Abandoned Quarry.

The easiest way to do this was by quad bike. Excited by this prospect, Foxy had a few goes at driving. It was not as easy as he had first assumed. Skidding if he turned too fast, stalling if he was too slow, at last he got the hang of it.

Mr. Keeper showed him a longer route to the quarry via a track through woods, bridleways and round the edges of some fields. This way Foxy did not have to go over stiles or through rusted gates.

Foxy felt very important driving the quad bike around and very responsible to be in charge of all these tools. Mr. Keeper was trusting him: this had never happened to Foxy before. No one had ever given him responsibility and believed he could follow through and complete a task successfully.

The tools were to be stored in a cavern at the base of the cliff. Looking after them and making sure they were kept secure and in good condition was another of Foxy's tasks.

Preparations completed, it was now time for Foxy to start work clearing the whole area.

The first problem Foxy had to contend with was the removal of any rubbish which had accumulated there. Fortunately, the quarry was too far from anywhere for fly tippers to jettison their rubbish. There was quite a lot of litter such as crisp packets, chocolate wrappers, empty plastic bottles, and other papery bits and pieces which had either been dropped or thrown away by the more adventurous rambler (who really should have known better) or had been tossed and blown by the wind . These had to be picked up and put into the black rubbish bags which Mr. Keeper had given Foxy, who wore blue plastic gloves while he retrieved some very disgustingly dirty pieces. But he was thankful he didn't have to remove broken sofas or old refrigerators and dumps of old building materials, which usually can be found in irresponsible fly tipping.

He had spent a couple of days doing this, and finally he had cleaned the area.

He surveyed the scene around him. Already it looked better, but there was a long way to go before he would feel satisfied with his work.

The rest of the tools he needed had been stored and hidden away at the back of a small cave at the edge of the quarry. Foxy decided the cavern was not a secure enough place to store this valuable equipment. There were plenty of large rocks and stones covering the floor of the cave. If he cleared these, he thought to himself, he could construct a bothie out of stones. He would make a door and would be able to lock all the equipment safely inside. So that is what Foxy did.

Foxy looked up and down the steep sides of The Abandoned Quarry. "Oh, this is going to be very hard work!" he muttered to himself.

Chapter Two

The Project

Horton was up and about early. He had congratulated himself after apprehending that villain, Foxy, and was delighted when villagers came and patted him on the back. But after a while he was beginning to get bored and needed a project to keep himself and his friends occupied.

Dressed in his red shorts and T shirt, he decided to wander over towards his BFF Morton's house in Dingley Dell. As he did so, he passed Foxy's door in the tree, leading to his underground den.

"I wonder what Foxy's doing now for his community service?" he asked himself.

"Morton! Are you in?" he shouted at Morton's back gate.

"Yes! I'm just doing some sorting out!" came the muffled reply from the shed.

“Come in and we’ll have a glass of lemonade.”

“I just came past Foxy’s place, and I was wondering how he’s getting on. Have you any idea what he’s up to?” Horton enquired.

When Morton replied that he didn’t have a clue, Horton’s mind set to work.

“I think it’s time we found out,“ mused Horton. “For the good of the community.“

The community weren’t bothered, now that the thief in their midst had been caught and dealt with, and they knew they were safe.

 Horton was curious.

The Robinettes and even The Tweets didn’t know, and they would have been the first to hear any tittle tattle at The Hall.

Horton and Morton decided they would find out.

The following morning, they got up bright and early. Horton didn't take long to dress himself in clean red T shirt and shorts and tie his red bandanna with white spots around his head. It took Morton longer to get ready. He put on his blue T shirt and blue shorts and put his blue baseball cap, with holes in it for his ears to go through, back to front on his head. Before that, he had put product on his hair to stop it sticking up and had moisturised his face.

At last they were both ready, so grabbing hold of their rucksacks, Horton's red 'Just In Case' one with all the essentials in it, including munchies and a drink, and Morton's blue 'Everything In It' one with all his bits and pieces, they began to put Horton's plan into action.

It was still very early when they hid behind some large oaks in Dingley Dell Woodlands from where they could see Foxy's home. He appeared wearing brown dungarees and an old brown flat cap, carrying a bag with thermos flask and a sandwich box poking up through the top. Horton winked at Morton. It was time to follow Foxy.

They followed him at a distance, making sure they kept him always in their sight. Foxy really was walking at a fast pace, and sometimes the two pals had to run and jump to keep up with him. Going through the rusty kissing gates was quite an obstacle as they creaked and banged as they went through. And there was the occasional time when Foxy stopped and looked back as he thought he had heard someone following him.

Eventually Foxy reached The Abandoned Quarry and disappeared inside the cave. Horton and Morton looked at each other.

"What's he doing in there? "they wondered. Their question was answered quickly, as Foxy came out holding a key and went over to what looked like a pile of stones. He disappeared inside and appeared wearing bright yellow ear defenders, large goggles, thick gloves and a big brush cutter attached to his chest by a wide strap. They watched entranced as Foxy began to climb the steep side at the left of the quarry. Once he had reached the top, they could hear the steady loud thrum of the brush cutter as it cut its way through the undergrowth as Foxy made his way carefully down. Their ears hurt with the noise and it had startled them.

"What is this place? "Morton whispered

"I don't know. I've never been here before!" replied Horton hoarsely, even though they had both lived all their lives in the area. His eyes took in the scene before them.

A high, white, sheer cliff face rose above them, its face streaked with a few overhanging plants and bushes. At each side, a steep slope covered with ash and beech trees and heavy undergrowth and brambles swept down to the base where they were hidden behind a large granite boulder. Foxy was steadily making his way down with his brush cutter, clearing the ground as he did so.

"What a magical place!" whispered Horton, slightly more loudly than he intended.

 At that point, there was a lull in the spitting and crackling of the brush cutter. Foxy looked up, and caught sight of the red T shirt and shorts and the blue T shirt and shorts.

"Hey! What are you doing down there? Are you spying on me? Has Mr. Keeper sent you?"

Embarrassed that they had been discovered, the friends stood up.

"No. Nothing like that!" cried Horton. "We were being nosey! We wondered what you were doing, so followed you here. What is this place? It's amazing!"

Foxy carefully made his way to the base of the cliff, took off his paraphernalia and placed the brush cutter on the floor. He explained that Mr. Keeper had given him this enormous task of clearing The Abandoned Quarry, left to the elements for a century or more. Once an important part of The

Hall's estate, it had been neglected, and Foxy had been given the job of clearing it up. It was a secret as people had forgotten about it and only wildlife and serious walkers knew it was there.

While Foxy was telling them this, Horton's 'I was Thinking' mind was racing ahead. Wasn't this an ideal place to have an adventure playground? Just think what they could do with all this space!

"If we gave you a hand, you wouldn't let on to Mr. Keeper, would you? And we promise we won't tell a soul. It would be our secret!" Horton said to Foxy and Morton.

He went on to explain his latest new project, which he had only just come up with.

Each day Foxy set off for The Abandoned Quarry.

As he passed The Hall, he made sure he said "Good Morning" to Mr. Keeper and Hardip who were putting CCTV cameras and installing a Burglar Alarm system throughout The Hall and its outbuildings. Mr. Keeper was very busy as this was a most important job following the thought that there could have been robbers in the vicinity. Sir had instructed him not to delay with its installation.

Mr. Keeper had been so impressed with Hardip's handiwork during the execution of Horton's plan to capture the thieves at The Hall, he had invited him to give him a helping hand.

Foxy thought that if he showed himself to Mr. Keeper in the morning and explained what he had done when he passed in the afternoon, that Mr. Keeper would be kept well informed and not have to worry about going out of his way to the Abandoned Quarry. There were two reasons for this: the first, that Mr. Keeper would not ask difficult questions;and, secondly, it would give Mr. Keeper time to complete other, more important jobs with his new assistant, Hardip. Foxy had definitely convinced himself that this was the right approach to keeping Horton's plan a secret.

Horton and Morton did not want to be seen, so they had examined a map and also googled waytogo.com and found another forgotten route to the quarry which bypassed The Hall. Each day they left early taking their sandwich boxes and flasks of drink in their rucksacks. Because they were working outdoors amidst thick undergrowth, they had foregone their usual coloured shorts and, like Foxy, wore dungarees. Naturally, Horton wore red dungarees and Morton blue ones.

The First Aid kit in Horton's red Just in Case rucksack was becoming depleted as plasters and small bandages found their way onto the friends' fingers and hands. Foxy did not allow them to use some of the machinery and equipment as they had not done a safety course as he had, but they cleared away all the vegetation which had been cut down, bringing it to a central point on the flat ground at the bottom of the cliff. The work was very arduous. They were hot and sweaty, and flies buzzed around them attracted by their perspiration. It was an Indian summer, and, even for October, it was like a summer's day.

Sometimes they looked like windmills as their flailing arms swept around in circles to swat the insects which appeared in swarms from the undergrowth. .

Each day, when they had finished, they all looked at the progress they had made and were well chuffed with themselves.

Each day, they returned home exhausted using the same route they had taken in the morning.

 Every afternoon, Foxy would go out of his way to say "Good Evening "to Mr. Keeper and describe his day's efforts. He would tell him of the debris that had been moved and how he had accumulated it at the base of the cliff. He would describe how he had coppiced and pruned the shrubs, ash and beech trees on the slopes. What Foxy did not say was about the help he was having from Horton and Morton.

When the weather eventually turned bad. Foxy would turn up in his brown mac and wellingtons; Horton in his red raincoat and hood; and Morton in his blue one with a rain hat. Wet lunchtimes would find the three huddled inside the small bothie Foxy had built. It was large enough to accommodate the three of them and warmer and more comfortable than sitting on the floor of the cave. Here they could have some respite from the occasional downpours and even from blustery storms with deafening thunder and shooting lightening. Fortunately, days like these were very few and far between. Nothing was going to deter them from the task they had set themselves.

The villagers and even their friends did not bother too much that the pals always seemed to be out. They were an adventurous pair who had always loved exploring, so their absence did not seem strange or their behaviour odd. Even Pinkie did not question their whereabouts: she was busy stocktaking in her fancy dress agency with the help of The Robinettes, who were missing their friends, The Tweets, who had migrated to warmer climes.

The only one who wondered what everyone was doing was Digby, and occasionally he would sneak out and follow the three, and watched and waited but could not figure out what they were up to. He could see they were working hard, and that was not something he really wanted to be involved in!

Chapter Three

The Grand Opening

Finally, their work was done. The sawing and hammering; the nailing and screwing; the sandpapering and painting had come to an end. They looked at their calloused hands. They looked around at their handiwork. They were all satisfied.

Now it was time to organise a Grand Opening for Horton's project, but only for their trusted friends!

The Robinettes would take messages to Ernie, the Sheep, and Corwen, the black Dexter Cow, as they were situated the most distant and it could take some time to find them as they were never in the same place.

Horton would invite Pinkie himself and Morton would speak to Hardip. The Robinettes were under strict orders not to divulge the secret to anyone up at The Hall but Digby (to be distinguished from

Monty, his identical twin, by the wearing of a red collar).

The following day was warm and sunny, ideal for the inauguration of Horton's project.

Ernestine arrived from across the fields, sporting her straw hat with a bright yellow flower, which she had picked en route. Corwen was with her as they had met on the way. Her rainbow coloured scarf cut quite a dash and the cowbells swung melodiously around Corwen's neck as they carefully wound their way to the base of the cliff at The Abandoned Quarry.

 Pinkie wore a pink silk Princess dress which almost reached down to the ground, a silver tiara on her head, and arrived sitting on Digby's shiny black shoulders. He had left his white naval jacket with the gold epaulettes and the gold anchor buttons at The Hall , fearing they might get dirty, but wore his captain's hat, as this was a very special day after all.

Hardip arrived on his little orange bicycle, wearing his orange helmet and orange safety sash. In his bicycle bag, he carried his Zorro costume into which he changed as soon as he arrived at the quarry. He had completed the task of helping Mr. Keeper put CCTV cameras around The Hall and its outbuildings. Mr. Keeper had given him a day off, as he was now officially employed as a jack of all trades helping around The Hall.

Horton and Morton had arrived earlier to welcome their friends. What else would they be wearing but their Zorro outfits?

Foxy also arrived early in his best brown velvet suit and brown trilby, and carried a large brown apron as he had been instructed to prepare the barbecue.

Foxy felt very important as he was the only one who had completed the health and safety course.

The Robinettes swooped in behind Pinkie and Digby occasionally flying so low that they nearly made Pinkie fall off Digby's back.

When the friends had all arrived, they stood mesmerised looking at The Abandoned Quarry which they had never realised had existed. Their eyes were like saucers, their mouths wide open. Even Digby, who had watched some of the progress, had never imagined it would look like this.

None of them expected to see anything of this proportion.

 The scene before them was one of enchantment, a magical wonderland.

A sailing ship, complete with masts and wooden steering wheel, port holes and decks and thick swinging ropes, appeared to be sailing out from a cave. Above it on a steep slope stood a castle with turrets and windows and crenulations, almost camouflaged by an enormous spider's web in the middle of which was trapped an enormous red dragon. There were swings, climbing nets, a towering fort with climbing tower, a tree top challenge with swinging logs and trails high up in the trees, an old gypsy caravan, wigwam dens made out of sticks. And the crowning glory was the long Zip wire which stretched from the top to the bottom of cliff with mattresses placed in just the right place to end the descent.

This was an adventure playground to feed the imagination!

What fun could be had here!

Foxy, true to his newly assumed responsibilities, had also ensured that as many safety requirements as possible had been met.

When they had all regained their composure and praised the three, Horton, Morton and Foxy for their spectacular work, it was time to test everything.

Amidst the laughter, screams and yells they all had a magnificent time.

Corwen on the Zip wire, her scarf streaming out behind her and cowbells clanging loudly caused some alarm but she landed safely, thrilled with this new experience.

Ernie could be seen dangling from the coiled ropes on the enormous sailing ship, swinging to and fro as she tried to catch hold of one of the wooden masts.

Pinkie had found her natural position as a Princess at the top of the castle, crying "Help! Save me from the Dragon!" while the three Zorro's climbed up the climbing tower in the fort to rescue her, and Digby was circling like a whirling dervish in front of the dragon.

The Robinettes flew swooping and looping from one friend to the other, chattering excitedly "What a wonderful time we're all having!"

Suddenly there was a Boing. Boing, Boing noise.

They immediately stopped what they were doing and eyes turned towards the sound.

Foxy had decided to try out the trampoline, which had been disguised as a large rock. There he was jumping high into the air, sit ups and somersaults no problem. They all clapped and cheered him in encouragement.

Eventually, they all heard their tummies rumbling. They hadn't noticed the time flying past. Foxy had completed his trampolining and was preparing the barbecue. The smell of sizzling sausages, burning burgers and frying onions wafted through the air. Chicken kebabs with mushrooms, courgettes and peppers were barbecuing slowly. Drinks were poured.

The friends settled down to devour their food. They really were hungry, and when they were all completely full, and the sun was beginning to sink lower in the sky, they decided, one and all, that it was, unfortunately, time to return home.

Foxy made sure that the fire for the barbecue was completely extinguished.

They all trudged home slowly; even Hardip didn't have the energy to pedal his bike. Exhaustion had overcome them.

What a fabulous time they had all had! Congratulations to Foxy, Horton and Morton!

Chapter Four

Disaster

Meanwhile, tensions had been rising at The Hall.

Sir and Milady had begun worrying about how they could make improvements and keep The Hall in a good state of repair, especially since the snoopers from the bank had been caught. There was no way that Sir Thomas Bunglebury (to give him his full title) would hand over the keys of Bunglebury Hall to the bank, or anyone else for that matter. He had the responsibility of keeping it in the Bunglebury Family, as it had been for centuries, and should be, for centuries to come.

Everything came to a head one day, not long after Horton and his friends had had their wonderful day out at The Abandoned Quarry.

Drip. Drip. Drip, drip, drip ……. The storm outside had not abated.

Sir heard the drips and climbed into the loft again, carrying a steel bucket. That made five large metal buckets he had placed under the leaking roof.

"How long would it last?" he wondered to himself.

With that thought still in his head. there was a crash in the bedroom. The noise reverberated through The Hall. The Robinettes, who had taken the place of the migratory Tweets, flew off the telephone wire in alarm. Horton, who had been drinking hot chocolate in the kitchen with Mrs. Keeper to escape from the heavy downpour, leapt up immediately and bounded upstairs.

"I'm coming!" he shouted.

He saw the ladder leading into the attic and carefully edged his way to the top. Sir was yelling at the top of his voice. Only Sir's head and shoulders and outstretched arms could be seen hanging on to the planks around what appeared to be an enormous hole. Horton leant out to grab the hands, but he was too late. Horton looked aghast as Sir disappeared, just his fingertips observable on the attic floor,or what was left of it.

Milady rushed upstairs.

She flung open a door. Dust and plaster covered the floor, the bed and all the bedroom furniture. It was as though someone had taken a huge tin of talcum powder, and scattered it, without a care in the world, all over the room. Her eyes went upwards. Two shoes covered with white dust, a pair of legs dangling from the ceiling, swinging backwards and forwards and Sir 's top half of his body clinging onto the remains of the attic floor for dear life and shrieking "Get me down! Get me down!"

Too late!

Not even Horton could save from his fate and Milady watched in astonishment as Sir bounced down onto the enormous bed, and after a couple of springs twanged noisily, he lay flat on his back like a ghost, covered from head to foot in broken plaster and dust.

Although it was a disaster, Milady couldn't help seeing the funny side. She sank to the floor and howled with laughter until she cried. Horton and Mrs. Keeper, who had also reached the bedroom by this time, also joined in laughing until tears rolled down their cheeks looking at Sir's ridiculous plight.

Something had to be done as a matter of urgency.

The rain had stopped.

Horton and Mrs. Keeper had returned to finish their hot chocolate in the kitchen, while Milady ran a hot soothing bubble bath to give Sir some time to recover from his accident. After a flurry of activity while The Robinettes flew around frantically saying "What a to do! What a to do!" about Sir's attic disaster, they settled back down at the listening post along the telephone wire attached to the wall next to the drainpipe.

Suddenly there was frantic activity as the wire swayed violently back and forth. It was like balancing on a circus tightrope as The Robinettes were bounced up and down, so agitated were they by what was happening inside The Hall.

This was unheard of. Never before had The Robinettes witnessed……………..A QUARREL! If only The Tweets were here!.

Sir and Milady were having an argument.

"There's nothing for it," Milady announced sharply. "We'll just have to sell some of Nicholas Hilliard's gold work, and that Flemish artist, what's her name? Ah yes, I remember, Levina Teerlinc. Some of her miniatures. "

"We can't do that! "responded Sir angrily. "These things have been in the family since Queen Elizabeth the First's time; since the first Sir Thomas Bunglebury was given The Hall!"

"Well, you come up with a better idea!" shouted Milady, as she flounced out of the sitting room.

The more she had studied the accounts, the more anxious she had become.

They had to save The Hall. But how?

If the roof wasn't fully repaired, the place would go to rack and ruin. Then where would they be? And the immediate issue had to be the repair of the bedroom ceiling.

It had become increasingly clear that they had a huge problem. It was almost as though they had been like ostriches, burying their heads in the sand, and just carrying on every day regardless of the repairs and renovations that were required to keep The Hall habitable.

So many people depended on them.

Choices had to be made; decisions taken; and they would need the support of the villagers of Bunbury if they were going to succeed.

First, they had to inform Mr. and Mrs. Keeper and old Ted the Gardener of their worries. They were aware of the situation: they had seen it coming.

Horton had left The Hall before the argument had begun. He was already thinking about how he and his friends could help to repair the holes in the leaking roof and patch up the bedroom ceiling.

The Robinettes were extremely distressed by the quarrel. "What a to do! What can we do?" they anxiously discussed between themselves.

Only one person they could think of might have some idea. "Horton! We must talk to Horton!" They all flew over to 5, Willow Wood Cottage where Horton was sitting at his table, head in his hands, trying to come up with a workable plan to repair the bedroom ceiling and attic floor. They arrived in agitation and all gabbled at once. He was very distressed that Sir and Milady, that most steadfast of couples, had had a quarrel This was unheard of!

"You must all stay calm," Horton advised. "Spreading worry and rumours will cause everyone more anxiety. I will go back to The Hall and find out what is happening."

Horton always said the right thing and calmed the atmosphere down.

When Horton arrived back at The Hall, The Robinettes resumed their positions as listeners and messengers.

 Sir and Milady had had an urgent meeting with Mr. and Mrs. Keeper and Ted the Gardener. They informed Horton that they had decided that the best way forward was to call a village meeting and have a public consultation. The interconnection between Bunglebury Hall and Bunbury was, after all, very close.

Digby and Monty had been so flummoxed by all that was going on, they kept springing up and rushing around in circles, first going in one direction and then the other until they exhausted themselves and flumped down in front of the fireplace. Digby was very relieved to see his friend Horton had arrived: they could all move forward instead of going round and round in circles.

The local radio made an announcement, and Mr. Keeper put up posters in the Village Memorial Hall and The Hare Inn, formerly known as The Bunglebury Arms, which had changed its name in honour of the heroic deeds of Horton for catching the thieves in their whereabouts. Mrs. Keeper gave one to Mrs. Tibbles at the local shop, and asked Mrs. Newhouse to tell her customers as she went delivering eggs.

SAVE THE HALL

PUBLIC CONSULTATION

Everybody is invited to attend this very important meeting.

Village Memorial Hall, Bunbury

6.00 p.m.

Wednesday, 23rd April.

"What's this? What's this!" everyone asked.

It was such a rare event for the owners of The Hall

to call a public meeting: so rare,that one had never

been called before!

Rumours were flying!

Chapter Five

The Meeting

As everyone arrived at the meeting Mr. Keeper handed everyone a copy of The Agenda. It was his job to make sure the rules for holding the meeting were followed correctly. This was too important a decision for there to be any mistake in the protocol. Everyone should be allowed to have their say; it had to be democratic, but it also had to be orderly and fair.

AGENDA.

1) Minutes arising from the last meeting. (None, as this was the first.)
   a) Apologies for absence. Great Aunt Willehelmina could not attend because of a prior engagement.
   b) Chairman's Address. Sir, of The Hall, would address the villagers.
2) Treasurer's Accounts. Milady was the treasurer.
3) Questions and Any Other Business.

There was a large turnout. No one could remember when a meeting had been called before. This must be very important, so everyone who could go, went.

As the villagers went in, they found themselves a seat on chairs placed in rows inside the hall. They looked onto a stage with five interlocking chairs in front of the closed, black curtains which hid the gymnastics equipment for the village Gym Club.

The Village Memorial Hall was full, and many had to stand at the back as there weren't enough chairs. They all had worried looks on their faces. Their livelihoods could be at stake for they were all involved with The Hall in one way or another. Horton and his friends had arrived early and found themselves spaces at the front near the stage. The hall became very noisy as they all talked amongst themselves.

Sir took his seat in the middle of the stage with Mr. Keeper and Ted the Gardener either side of him. Milady and Mrs. Keeper sat at each end.

Mr. Keeper stood up and thanked everyone for coming, once everyone in the Memorial Hall had settled down and the noise had subsided. He said there were no minutes from any previous meetings, as this was the first; then he apologised on Great Aunt Wilhelmina's behalf for her absence.

He asked Sir to now give The Chairman's address, and sat down as Sir stood up.

Firstly, Sir thanked Horton, ably assisted by Morton, Hardip and Digby for catching the thieves who they had thought were going to rob The Hall. He told the assembled group that the two men apprehended had not, in fact, been robbers, but had been sent by the bank. It was now necessary that if they did not want The Hall to be repossessed by the bank, they desperately needed to raise some, or rather, quite a lot of, money.

At this point Milady, as treasurer, stood up to give some details. She thanked Mrs. Keeper for selling cakes, chutneys and preserves at Mrs. Tibbles' shop. Mrs. Keeper patted her short, greying, wavy hair with pride; her red cheeks turned even more lobster scarlet and she began wringing her chubby hands together in her lap. Ted the Gardener was praised for selling fruit, vegetables and flowers from the walled garden at The Hall. (Ted felt very proud to be mentioned and stood up from his seat, looking unusually tidy wearing a belt around his trousers instead of his usual piece of string, bowed and sat back down again.)

"Unfortunately, "she said," this is not enough to cover all the expenses. We would be grateful if you could come up with some ideas to raise money. We know how important The Hall is to everyone here, and we don't want to do anything which could have a detrimental effect on you and the village."

Everyone looked very perplexed. They talked amongst themselves. What could be done? Did anyone have any ideas?

After some minutes of rumbling discussion around the room, Horton stood up and looked at all the crestfallen faces.

Everyone gasped!

Would Horton have a brainwave?

Would he be the hero of the hour again?

Horton began "I Was Thinking. "

The villagers looked at each other knowingly and raised their eyebrows in expectation.

"I have a confession to make, "he continued.

Oh no! What on earth would such a valiant and honest person have to confess in front of so many people.? The tension in the room was palpable.

 "My best friend Morton and I have been helping Foxy."

Muttering came from the audience. Was Foxy the type of company an upstanding member of the community like Horton should keep?

" Mr. Keeper gave Foxy the task of clearing The Abandoned Quarry, which some of you older residents may remember, fell into disuse a long time ago. I'm afraid Mr. Keeper that I came up with a project for my own and my friends' satisfaction. Morton and I followed Foxy to his work one day. We just were curious to know what task he had been set. After seeing the place, I'm afraid I had an idea to turn it into an adventure playground for myself and my friends."

This was preposterous. Horton. keeping a secret and making use of the land for his own ends.

Horton continued, " I know it was bad of me, but people had forgotten about it and it was the ideal place to have some fun. I swore Foxy to secrecy in return for helping him clear the area. Foxy did all the hard work with the equipment, as he knew the health and safety regulations, and Morton and I cleared it all up with him. I do feel very ashamed of keeping this secret from Mr. Keeper, but he was so preoccupied with all the work at The Hall and we really didn't think it was worth bothering him. I wonder now if it would be of any help to open it for everybody's use, and maybe charge a small fee."

Horton felt it was the longest speech he had ever made, and it was also a confession.

How would Sir and Mr. Keeper take it? It was an admission to trespassing, and Foxy and Morton were his accessories.

Then Hardip stood up, holding his orange bicycle helmet in his hand.

" If Sir would allow people to see his vintage car and motorbike collection," he began, and pushed his spectacles up higher on his nose apprehensively.

Hardip was being very presumptive. There was a gasp around the room.

Sir's vintage car and motorbike collection had been started by his great grandfather and continued by Sir's grandfather and father. It was a collection comparable to the finest one owned by Lord Montague at Beaulieu. Surely Hardip wasn't going to suggest that Sir sold it. "As I said, if Sir opens it up to the public, I would be happy to donate my collection of antique headwear to The Hall, " he finished. "Also," he added, rather embarrassingly, "the adventure playground really is an extraordinary feat of ingenuity!"

Everyone knew how much Hardip loved his hat collection and had even extended his Hatter's Cottage to accommodate them all. This was a very fine gesture.

Horton stood up again. "So, we could use the vintage car and motorbike collection, and the Adventure Playground to attract a wide range of visitors to The Hall," he suggested.

Mr. Keeper was not very impressed, and as Horton was talking his eyes searched the room for Foxy.

Foxy, looking very smart in his brown velvet jacket was standing just inside the door, trying to be inconspicuous. When Mr. Keeper caught sight of him, he wagged his index finger of his right hand at him and shook his head. But his eyes were smiling.

"It really is magnificent and great fun" shouted Hardip, Pinkie. Digby, Ernestine and Corwen in chorus, as they had all made great efforts to attend such an important meeting.

Even The Robinettes performed flying dances around the room in agreement.

Horton looked anxiously around the room to see what impact he had made. The whole community was smiling. They liked what they had heard.

"Well done, Horton!"

"You've come up trumps!"

"Brilliant idea!"

These were just a few of the comments.

When the cheering and clapping for Horton and Hardip died down, Milady stood up and said "Great ideas. And I think we should open The Hall and grounds to visitors from outside Bunbury, like Chatsworth and Castle Howard and other estates do, so that everyone can enjoy it and this will also help pay for The Hall's refurbishment. This could benefit the whole community."

As she sat down, the interlocking chairs rocked to and fro slightly but no one took any notice.

Then Mrs. Keeper leapt up, still scarlet faced and wringing her chubby hands with excitement to exclaim "That's a fantastic idea!"

 The five chairs were completely unbalanced and they, together with their occupants disappeared backwards and downwards. All that could be seen were the closed black curtains disarranged, swishing at the back of the stage and three pairs of shoes and one odd one attached to eight legs waving around in the air. One, a pair of red high heels, which matched Milady's red skirt and jacket; one pair of brown laceups belonging to Mr. Keeper; one pair of green wellington boots on Ted the Gardener's feet; and one brown Brogue and one brown and orange sock with the word Wednesday on it with a big toe sticking through a hole at the top belonging to Sir.

After a shocked momentary silence, the hall burst into uproar with great mirth and laughter, so ridiculous a sight was before them all. Horton rushed onto the stage and pulled back the curtains.

Thank heavens! No one was injured as they had fallen onto the mattresses belonging to the gym club.

As they all reappeared, red faced and with only their pride injured, and regained their composure,

Sir said "Well, I think our business here is concluded. Are there any further questions?"

One small hand went up at the back of the room. "That was funny! Could you do it again?"

Chapter Six

Decision Time

It was too late that evening for Mr. Keeper to go and see the changes to The Abandoned Quarry As he left the meeting, he managed to catch up with Foxy and asked him to meet him at the usual kitchen door entrance to The Hall the following morning. He also asked if Horton could come along as well.

At the appointed time, half past eight, the three of them set off for The Abandoned Quarry.

Mr. Keeper was feeling rather grumpy. The day had started grey and drizzly; his knees were aching because the weather had turned chilly; and he would much prefer to be working inside than bumping a long distance over a rutted path on the quad bike to see something which he had no doubt would turn out to be one of Horton's hare-brained schemes. And the immediate issue had to be the repair of the bedroom ceiling .

They didn't talk much on their way. Foxy and Horton hoped Mr. Keeper would have a huge surprise. And so, he did. For when they reached the quarry, there was a large carved wooden sign:

"Impressive!" thought Mr. Keeper; and as he walked under the sign and through the entrance, he was completely taken aback. He had never thought The Abandoned Quarry would look like this.

The wooden ship had been beautifully designed to appear as if it was coming out from the cavern, its masts tall and straight, ropes and netting dropping down to the gleaming deck, port holes for imaginary canons, even a plank for walking on and a trampoline, disguised as a rock, to land upon. Above it , on the steep slope, a castle, complete with turrets, crenellations and winding staircases, was hidden behind the most enormous spider's web camouflaging a magnificently terrifying red dragon with wings. A fort, wigwams made out of hazel sticks, swings, slides, a gypsy caravan: everything was here to inspire the imagination. What a wonderful creation!

He looked up to the top of the cliff. Was that really one of the longest zip wires he had ever seen?

And all finished to the highest quality! His heart swelled with pride. He felt he had taught Foxy well.

"Well! I never expected this!" exclaimed Mr. Keeper. "What an extraordinary achievement!"

"Do you think it could be used as part of The Hall's Open Day?" asked Horton quietly. He did not want to be disappointed.

"Oh, I think so! Most definitely! "responded Mr. Keeper. "But before I can give a definitive answer, it has to be checked over by the Health and Safety Executive. Only when we have a certificate from them can it be used by the public. From what I have seen though, I shouldn't think it will be a problem. "

There was one problem which Mr. Keeper could foresee. It was a long way from The Hall. Would people want to walk that far? He scratched his head. What could be done about that?

Horton put on his 'I Was Thinking' hat, which, of course wasn't a hat at all, but meant that he needed time to ponder this dilemma. He sat down on the ground and thought and thought. At last, an idea formed. "When the quarry was in use," he asked, "how did they get the material to and from it?"

"Ah yes!" replied Mr' Keeper. "They used the canal. That stretch of stagnant water alongside the path. If we could clear that, we could use a barge to carry visitors to Crusoe's Cavern!"

"That would be really exciting! "said Foxy.

Back at The Hall, there had been a lot of discussion going on.

You could see this by the frenetic activity of The Tweets, who had now returned from their winter migration, hopping and bouncing excitedly on the telephone wire. They all wanted to hear what was being said inside.

"I'm glad we got that sorted last night," Sir had begun.

"It's going to be a lot of work. "replied Milady "And the first thing we must sort out is who is going to open The Hall? We have to have a celebrity!"

"A celebrity!" bounced The Robinettes and The Tweets. "Awesome!"Could it be a pop star? Or perhaps Mary Berry: she had judged the village Bake Off, which Mrs. Keeper had sadly missed as Digby had absconded with her wicker basket of cakes? Or maybe a famous T.V. personality?

Surely, Sir and Milady wouldn't perform The Grand Opening themselves?

Speculation was rife. Names were bandied about.

Finally, it came down to a choice between two. Fenella Spruce was a forerunner as she hosted Antiques Down Your Way, and she would have a great crowd of followers who would be very interested in the history and the interesting valuables which Sir's ancestors had accumulated.

The other main choice was Guy Larkin, a funny character who spoke in a strange dialect but who loved all things technical and mechanical. He had a huge following of young and old, not only on television, but also on the racing circuits. Guy had fronted shows about engineering, trains and cars and who seemed to have an infinitesimal curiosity and knowledge about a wide range of subjects, including history.

"Guy Larkin! Guy Larkin!" bounced The Robinettes and The Tweets in unison on the telephone wire. Sir was also keen for Guy Larkin to be involved, as he would undoubtedly be fascinated by Sir's extensive collection of vintage vehicles housed in The Old Stables.

Even. though The Robinettes and The Tweets had nothing to do with the final choice, it was proposed that Guy Larkin would be invited to perform The Grand Opening.

The reasoning behind this choice was simple, Sir explained to Milady.

"Guy Larkin has knowledge about the construction of canals, which will be helpful. He also loves vintage vehicles, so can give us some useful tips. He is very approachable; men like him and women swoon over him. We will have to ask him if he could be sympathetic to our cause? Will he help? We can only ask!"

Guy Larkin was thrilled to be asked. Immediately he wanted to visit The Hall and acquaint himself with the place. But he didn't want the whole village to know. It was to be a visit in secret.

A date was quickly arranged. Guy Larkin arrived dressed in old work clothes. He was intrigued and ready for anything. Sir and Milady showed him around The Hall itself. What a place! And all those antiques! He particularly loved the collection of clocks.

Sir took him down to see his collection of vintage cars and motorbikes.

"My word! this is really impressive! I think it's even better than Lord Montague's collection at Beaulieu, down in the New Forest!"

Hardip smiled with pride. He was now helping to look after this collection and was putting a final polish on the Daimler, a similar one to that used by King George V, which was Sir's pride and joy. His technical understanding was increasing and he was helping to keep the vehicles in smooth running order.

"Do they work?" asked Guy."Of course!" replied Hardip, and instantly opened the door, glancing at Sir to make sure it was alright. After a short drive round the grounds in the Daimler, Mr. Keeper arrived at The Old Stables, which housed Sir's collection.

"There is something else we would like you to see," Sir said." It's quite a distance. I think we should ride on the quad bike."Taking the longer route to avoid the stiles and the kissing gates, the four bumped their way to The Abandoned Quarry, now renamed Crusoe's Cavern. Horton, Morton and Foxy were waiting for them there. After introducing them to Guy, Sir said "This used to be an old quarry, but these three have turned it into a magnificent Adventure Playground,"

"Wow! And you did all this by yourselves?"

The three nodded in reply.

"The only problem is it's a long way from The Hall and can be difficult to reach. We could have a solution, but it means some hard work and we would like your thoughts on its feasibility."

Guy followed them over to a footpath which lay alongside a stretch of stagnant water.

"A canal!" he exclaimed. "I see now! When the quarry was working, this is how they could get materials to and from it. If we renovated the canal, a boat could take passengers from the lake in front of The Hall and bring them to Crusoe's Cavern! Great for the children and as a picnic site. I'd love to help, if that's alright," he added.

So, it was with great delight that they accepted his kind offer. To be honest, this what was what they had all been hoping for.

Following Guy's instructions, Horton dressed in his red dungarees; Morton in his blue ones, Foxy, in his brown, and Hardip in orange dungarees, started work on clearing the canal. Mr. Keeper oversaw the work.

The past few weeks had been serious stuff. The end was in sight.

The Robinettes and some of The Tweets twirled around their heads singing encouraging songs as they cleared the debris and verdant growth away from the canal. The remaining Tweets retained their position on the telephone wire back at The Hall, just in case there was a problem which needed immediate attention.

Digby, wearing black dungarees, arrived carrying a basket of goodies provided by Mrs. Keeper, to keep their strength up.

Mr. Keeper observed they were doing so well. " You don't need me here. I can leave you to it and get on with something else!"

Horton whispered to The Robinettes: "Could you ask Pinkie if she would judge a competition? Could she come to my house when we get back about half past five, please? " The Robinettes were glad to help out.

So, as they threw the rubbish into wheelbarrows and bags, Horton pulled at a piece of wet greenery "Let's see who's the smelliest? " and threw a chunk at Morton . In retaliation, he grasped a fistful of mud and threw it back at Horton, Horton ducked and it hit Hardip full in the face, muddying his spectacles so that he couldn't see and fell into a pile of obnoxious smelling weed.

Foxy and Digby joined in and soon they all looked slimy green monsters from the deep; muddy and covered in green, disgusting smelling weeds.

What a messy, smelly fun fight!

Time was passing by. It was time to return home.

They cleaned themselves, and the towpath up as best they could. Digby even threw himself into the cleaned canal water, but as he climbed onto the bank, he shook himself violently to get dry. In so doing, the other four were even wetter and smellier than they were before. "How could you?" they shouted together.

Returning to Horton's cottage, Pinkie was waiting for them in her Red Riding Hood costume.

"You wanted me to judge a competition?" she asked Horton incredulously, seeing them all wet and dirty.

"Yes please," he replied. "Could you do a sniff test? Pinkie! Who's the smelliest of all of us?"

Pinkie laughed. "You're all disgusting! All of you need a bath!" She pinched her nose with her fingers." But I'll make the hot chocolate and marshmallows while you all get cleaned up!"

Whilst clearing and repairing the canal, Foxy had discovered an old barge hidden under layers of weeds and fallen leaves. They poured lots and lots buckets of water over it, and scrubbed and scrubbed it.

Once renovated and painted , Guy and Hardip restored it to water worthiness.

Now, looking like new with polished seats and smart royal blue and scarlet red paint, it was ready to take passengers from The Hall to Crusoe's Cavern.

Ted the Gardener made good use of the grass and weeds collected, turning them into excellent compost for his vegetable and flower gardens. The rest of the rubbish he put onto the bonfire. There was nothing Ted liked better than a good, controlled bonfire. He had learnt the hard way when he was younger.

Bonfires could easily get out of control and could burn down garden sheds and trees if you built them too close to them. Rather scary at the time, but Ted had learnt a lesson and fortunately no great harm had been done. If anyone wanted a big bonfire, Ted the Gardener was the person to ask.

Chapter Seven

Open Hall

Everything had seemed to have taken forever to get finished, but finally they were ready for The Grand Opening. The day chosen was the August Bank Holiday: a final fling of holiday mood before the summer ended.

Milady, Mrs. Keeper and a chorus of helpers had cleaned and polished and learnt as much as they could about all the history of The Hall and its antiques, to enable them to answer any questions.

Ted the Gardener and his groundsmen had tidied flower beds and cut the grass and had increased their knowledge of that great landscaper, Capability Brown, who had made the grounds into the marvellous parks they were.

Under Sir's and Hardip's eagle eyes, the car and motorbike collection had been cleaned and polished until they gleamed and sparkled.

Mr. Keeper, Foxy, Horton and his friends had been installing ice cream kiosks and a small café as well as cleaning up the barbecue and picnic area.

 Digby, with his twin Monty helping him, made sure that the boat was ready to sail.

When Mrs. Keeper wasn't working in the house, she could be found in the kitchen preparing and cooking a virtual feast for the stomach and the eyes.

 Sir had gone round the grounds offering to help put up marquees and tents. But all the stall holders were very wary. Wasn't his surname Bunglebury? Wasn't there a reason for that? They all knew the story of his ancestor, the first Sir Thomas Bunglebury? Hadn't it been a sheer fluke that he had fired the cannon and set fire to the lead galleon of the invading Spanish Armada and destroyed it completely, causing the remainder of the Spanish ships to turn tail and sail back to Spain as fast as they could? And wasn't the present Sir Thomas Bunglebury just like him; a disaster just waiting to happen though his intentions were good? No one wanted their marquee or tent to suddenly collapse in a gust of wind , because Sir had been distracted and moved, well meaning, to something else without tightening the guy ropes or pushing poles far enough into the ground. For all his kind thoughts and helpfulness, sometimes things are better left to the experts.

Guy Larkin arrived at The Hall smartly dressed for the occasion. Everyone was assembled at the front of The Hall. Sir handed Guy a pair of scissors.

"It gives me great pleasure to open this magnificent Bunglebury Hall!" and Guy cut the ribbon across the entrance.

The local brass band from neighbouring Gigglesworth struck up a merry medley. The small marquees housing the craft exhibitions opened their doors.

The delicious aroma of cakes, burgers and buns wafted around the grounds.

Petrol fumes from the old cars and motorbikes hung in the air.

Guy Larkin was in his element driving visitors around with Mr. Keeper in the vintage cars, while Hardip helped them choose the appropriate headgear and showed them the other cars and motorbikes in the garages.

Digby looked magnificent in his naval hat and white jacket with gold epaulettes and gold anchor buttons, steering the boat very steadily from the lake in front of The Hall along the canal to Crusoe's Cavern. There was a large queue of excited parents and children wanting to go there.

At Crusoe's Cavern, Foxy, in his best brown velvet jacket, was ensuring everyone kept to the safety rules and wore helmets and put on harnesses to come down the Zip Wire.

Pinkie, in a new pale blue Cinderella ball gown, and Ernestine with a matching beautiful blue flower in her battered straw hat, were patrolling the steep slope with the castle and fort and play areas; while Corwen with her rainbow coloured scarf and sporting her melodious cow bells, looked after the picnic area, ensuring picnickers used the litter bins and left no rubbish behind.

Morton, in his best blue T shirt and shorts, blue back to front baseball hat over his ears, his hair smoothed down with product, and his well moisturised face, watched over the ship. Horton, dressed in his red silk shirt and red velvet waistcoat sporting his gold Acme Thunderer whistle, his red and white spotted dicky bow and black trousers with the red satin stripe, oversaw the ice cream kiosks and was doing a roaring trade alongside the café. He would have preferred to be in his red T shirt and red shorts; that would have been more comfortable. Then again, he felt he needed to be distinguished on this first Open Day, and after much indecision, he finally succumbed to wearing his best clothes.

He surveyed the scene, waved at Foxy at the top of the cliff, and to the rest of his friends. What a valuable contribution they had made to the day! The visitors left. exhausted.

The helpers left, exhausted.

Clearing up would begin the following day.

Everything had been a great success. Even Fine Shine, cars washed and cleaned while you have fun, run by the local Scouts and Guide group, made bucketsful of money.

Sir, Milady, Mr. and Mrs. Keeper counted how much they had made. Would it be enough to repair the roof?

Milady kept the accounts. Income; expenditure. Everything had to be accounted for.

Horton felt he had neglected his own place during this eventful time, and was delighted to be working again in his own cottage, in his old clothes; occasionally relaxing in his red deckchair in his beautiful garden, harvesting his own vegetables.

Time to relax!

His friends were relaxing too after all the frenetic activity. Only Hardip, who was now working up at The Hall; and Foxy, who still had some of his

Community service to be completed were not relaxing at every opportunity.

Even Digby, who had been praised to the hilt for his excellent boating and steering skills, was settled in front of the fireplace curled up by his twin, Monty, who had worked by his side on the boat.

Finally, the money had been counted. It was time to call another meeting at The Village Memorial Hall.

As before, notices were placed around Bunbury; one at the village hall itself, one in Mrs. Tibbles' shop; one at The Hare Inn and Mrs. Newhouse, who had done tremendous business at The Open Day, took messages round to both her old and new customers.

This time it was decided that an Agenda was not required.

This time the chairs onstage were not interlocked. Although the community had enjoyed the spectacle of the back flips, those involved in that exhibition had no wish to repeat it.

When everybody was seated or had found a space to stand and was quiet, Sir stood up. "Thank you all for coming tonight; and we would like to thank you all for the magnificent way you have helped The Hall."

The audience looked at each other with wide smiles and applause.

"Milady will now give you a rundown of the accounts."

Milady stood up and explained how much it had cost to run the Open Day, and then gave an account of how much each of the different activities had made. It was a staggeringly large amount in total, but Crusoe's Cavern with the boat ride had far exceeded any expectations. In fact, the total meant that the renovation repair to The Hall's roof could go ahead without delay.

Everyone cheered! This was such good news!

The Hall had been saved from rack and ruin and from the grips of the bank.

What a relief!

It had also brought lots of sightseers into the village. No longer did they park their cars in the car park belonging to The Hall and follow waytogo.com's route to the local beauty spot. They parked went into Bunbury; they bought Bunbury buns; the local eggs; the local arts and crafts and, of course, The Hall, its vintage car and motorbike collection and the Adventure Playground were at the top of the list of attractions. The village thrived.

And Horton,' I Was Thinking' Horton , had really saved The Hall .

Horton , you're a hero!

EPILOGUE

'Horton becomes a Hero'

Horton had not been born a hero.

He had never had any ambition to be a hero. His clear and quick thinking had catapulted him into the role of Hero.

The recognition that Horton had received following his saving of Sir Thomas Bunglebury from drowning in the canal,was flattering enough. Further to his exploits to catch the thieves who were causing alarm to the residents of both The Hall and the village, and the major part Horton had played in rescuing Bunglebury Hall from ruination had turned him into a revered local Hero.

Horton was modest in his acceptance of this role, but Sir wanted to mark Horton's position as a local hero. To do this, Sir had placed a wooden sculpture of two boxing hares in an inconspicuous place in The Hall's car park.

The inauguration had been attended by Horton and Morton, who were thrilled by the inscription at the base: Horton and his BFF Morton, who saved Sir Thomas Bunglebury from drowning. Also present were: Sir Thomas Bunglebury; his wife, Milady; Mr. and Mrs. Keeper; Ted the Gardener ; Digby, and his twin brother Monty; Pinkie; Hardip; Ernestine the sheep; Corwen, the black Dexter cow; Mrs. Newhouse; Mrs. Tibbles from the Grocery Shop. They had all stood and cheered under the large, spreading oak tree by the rambling hedge, just to the left of the car park entrance to Bunglebury Hall.

In the future, only a few inquisitive visitors to The Hall , or ramblers out on a day's walk following routes marked out on waytogo.com's website would notice the wooden sculpture. They would wander over and read the inscription. Who were

these characters, they might wonder?

The most curious would want to find out more, and

would also try to discover what Horton and his BFF

were doing now!

From the author

Dear Reader,

If you enjoyed reading this book, I hope you will like the next in the series. Here is a short preview. Keep reading!

Nicky Lyng

THE HORTON CHRONICLES
ONCE A HERO, ALWAYS A HERO.

Sto… *(Crackle, Hiss)* …. Stu… *(Crackle, Hiss)*

……**Sta**…. *Crackle, Hiss) …Mmmmmmmm.*

These were the stuttering words Horton heard in telephone call from Old Bert, The Station Master at Bunbury Halt, as the call hissed and crackled and finally broke up.

The band was due soon to play at The Winter Concert.

There must be a problem……

EXTRAS!

Do <u>you</u> want to know more?

> ➤ **Perhaps you like maps. Included in this section are a map of the Bunglebury Hall estate and a map of Bunbury Village.**

> ➤ **Or are you interested in websites? A copy of the Waytogo.com website entitled BUNBURY VILLAGE can be found here..**

> ➤ **Do you want to discover more about the history and development of Bunglebury Hall. The Timeline should be of help.**

Map of Bunglebury Hall and Estate- The ancesteral home of Sir Thomas Bunglebury.

Waytogo Tourist Map Bunbury Village

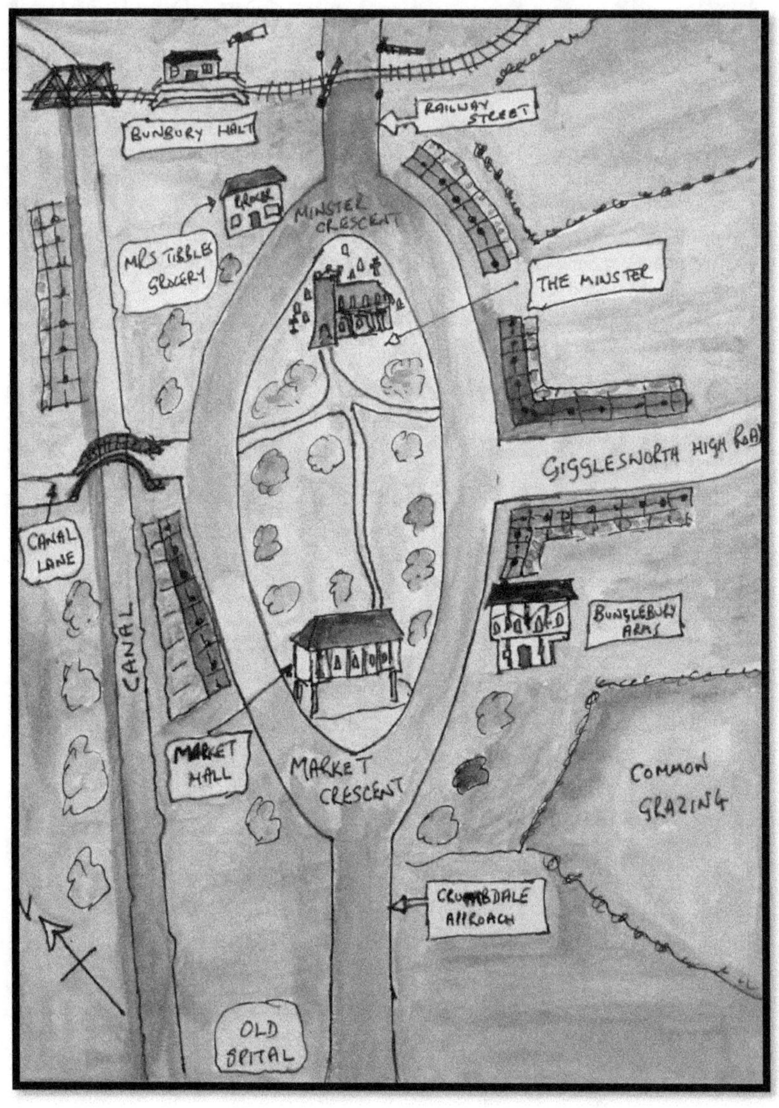

Bunbury Village ☆☆☆

Population: 613

The village is situated in an area of outstanding natural beauty in the West of England and is a walkers' paradise. Walks include limestone outcrops and escarpments and ancient Anglo-Saxon fields. The area is famous for blackberrying and its unspoilt canal and locks are a peaceful haven for boat lovers and fishing.

Within this beautiful setting the discerning traveller will find a place with great history , a local community bound together by friendship and camaderie which is welcoming to strangers from far and wide.

Local personalities

Sir Thomas Bunglebury

Owner of Bunglebury Hall a Sixteenth Century Manor House and descendent of a Hero of the Battle against the Spanish Armada (1588).

Lady Melody Bunglebury

Lady of the Manor of Bunglebury and married to Sir Thomas. Former renowned TV International and War Correspondent.

Horton the Hare

The most unassuming, modest and heroic of hares.

Guy Larkin

National celebrity, well known for his engineering skills and inventions. Sports enthusiast and challenge record breaker. Patron of Bunglebury Hall.

Mr Keeper

The Estate Manager of Bunglebury who with his wife Mrs Keeper manages all aspects of the Hall's maintenance and daily life. Trusted upstanding member of the community . Scout leader, chairman of the Village Hall Committee and events manager ,

The Crew

Horton's friends and associates who loyally support him in all his adventures. Including his BFF Morton, Corwen, Hardip,

Bunbury Market Hall Farmers' Market

Every Tuesday, Thursday and Saturday from 8.00 am until 12.30pm.

Fresh local vegetables and meat sourced organically. Freshy caught fish from the North Sea and Atlantic – Thursdays only

Hosiery stall and bric a brac.

*The Bunglebury Arms ***

Offers Bed and and Excellent Breakfast. Good home-cooked food prepared lunchtime and evenings.

Tel: 0765432198

Pinkerton's Fancy Dress Agency

By appointment only.

The Hollow, Dingley Dell, Woodlands.

Bunbury Village ☆☆☆

Population: 613

Bunbury is a small black and white timbered village dating from the Middle Ages.

The timbered and half timbered houses have black oak beams exposed on the outside and the walls in between are painted white.

One of the most significant structures is The Bunglebury Arms, an inn dating from 1589. Timber framed, this friendly hostelry provides good food and shelter for weary travellers.

Other noteworthy buildings are The Minster Church, with original stained glass window dating from the thirteenth century, and housing the tombs of Sir Thomas Bunglebury, the first owner of Bunglebury Hall gifted by Queen Elizabeth 1 in 1588, and his descendants.

The Minster

Monday, Wednesday and Friday

Matins (11.00 am) and Evensong (3.30pm)

Sundays Holy Communion 11.00 am

The Market Hall, a building used for the sale of animals and local products by farmers over the centuries; and The Grocery Shop and Bakery selling a variety of products including the famous Bunbury Buns.

For all your grocery and bakery needs, including the famous Bunbury Buns.

Go to Mrs Tibbles' Grocery Shop opposite the Minster, Bunbury.

Bunglebury Hall Historical timeline
Key Events

Date	National Events	Bunglebury Hall Events
1350		Baron Hottington, a wealthy wool merchant, buys farmland and constructs a grand manor house.
1558 →	Papal Bull decrees excommunication of Elizabeth And actively encourages plots against her for supporting Protestants. Jesuit priest Nicholas Owen, now patron Saint of Escapologists and illusionists, builds priest holes for Catholics	
1587		Hottington lands and house confiscated by Elizabeth1 for hiding Jesuit priests.

1588	Spanish Armada sails. Sir Francis Drake in command of English Navy.	Thomas Bunglebury fires cannonball from which The Silver Goose which sets alight arsenal aboard Spanish Flagship and destroys many of the Armada ships.
1589		Thomas Bunglebury knighted and given the Forfeited manor house and lands.
1603	Death of Elizabeth 1.	
1631		Inigo Jones, architect, and his nephew employed for building work at Bunglebury Hall.
1631 to 1695	Charles I, Cromwell Lord Protector, Charles 2, James 2	Changing of sides from Cavaliers to Roundheads, and Catholics to Protestants and back again
1689 to 1702	Mary daughter of James 2 co-ruler with her husband William 3 of Orange. Mary died in 1694	Avenues created in the Dutch style. Capability Brown designs landscapes for Bunglebury Hall.

1790→		Start of the Industrial Revolution Canal built to transport chalk and Limestone from Bunglebury Quarry Gigglesworth
1860s		Railway built to transport quarried Chalk and limestone from Bunbury Halt to Gigglesworth and Crumdale.
1900s		Closure of the Canal
1920s		Closure of the Quarry
Present day		Sir Thomas Bunglebury and his wife in Residence at Bunglebury Hall.